AMERICA'S
DAUGHTER

BOOKS BY CELESTE DE BLASIS

A Wild Hope
A Wild Heart
A Wild Legacy

AMERICA'S DAUGHTER

CELESTE DE BLASIS

bookouture

Published by Bookouture in 2021

An imprint of Storyfire Ltd.
Carmelite House
50 Victoria Embankment
London EC4Y 0DZ

www.bookouture.com

ISBN: 978-1-80019-326-0
eBook ISBN: 978-1-80019-325-3

BOOK I

MASSACHUSETTS AND VIRGINIA

Chapter 1

Boston, Massachusetts, December 16, 1773

It seemed as if all of Boston was at Old South Meeting House. People had started gathering hours before, and had continued to come in their thousands until Old South and the streets outside were packed solid.

Ariadne clutched her twin's hand so tightly, Adrian winced. "I am not going to lose you," he grumbled in her ear, "but if you don't loosen your grip, my hand is going to fall off."

Addie complied, but she didn't break contact. Suddenly their adventure didn't seem as good an idea as it had at the beginning. "Papa is going to lock us up forever if he discovers where we've been," she said.

"There is so much confusion at home, no one will know we're not there." Ad was fairly certain of that, but he shared his sister's tension. The crowd was growing restless, coiling with energy as if it were one great beast instead of separate souls. It was waiting for word that Governor Hutchinson had backed down from his resolve that the tea-bearing ships in the harbor not be allowed to leave without unloading their cargoes. The governor had gone so far as to order Admiral Montagu to block the harbor.

Ad studied the faces around him. He knew some of these people. He reminded himself that these were no more than the citizens of Boston, here to make known their latest grievance against a government in England that seemed determined to treat the colonists as less than Englishmen. Still, Boston had seen disturbances before, and not all had been harmless. He could hear his father's deep voice denouncing the actions of the mob, warning of the danger of "witless mechanics," common laborers who were pleased to defy the Crown's authority just for the sport of it. Three years before, people had died when soldiers had been provoked into firing on civilians. His father would never forgive him if anything happened to Addie.

"Perhaps we ought to go home now."

He had barely got the words out before Addie refused.

"No! We haven't found Justin or Silas yet. I know they're here, they must be. They wouldn't miss this."

Ad had a good idea of how angry Justin, their older brother, was going to be if he saw them, but he knew it was useless to protest further. Though he knew Addie understood his misgivings, she was determined to see this through; he could feel her stubbornness as if it were wrapped around her like a cloak.

And then the waiting was over. Francis Rotch, whose ship the *Dartmouth* had not been allowed to leave the harbor, had, at the request of the meeting's leaders, gone to appeal to the governor. Now it was six o'clock, and the captain returned to say that the governor would not relent.

Samuel Adams and his fellow lawyers, Josiah Quincy and John Rowe, had kept the crowd diverted, orating on the non-importation of certain British goods, specifically the tea in three recently arrived ships, but now Mr. Adams stepped into the pulpit and intoned, "This meeting can do nothing more to save the country."

The twins were outside Old South but near the door, and no one was taking particular notice of what appeared to be two stripling boys. The words rolled over them. Almost before the last syllable died, a war whoop sounded from outside, close by them, as if Adams' words had been a prearranged signal, and a band of men dressed as Mohawk warriors dashed past, down Milk Street, heading for Griffin's Wharf. "Boston Harbor is a teapot this night!" someone shouted.

The disguises of feathers, blankets, smeared faces, and night shadows were not deep enough to conceal Justin and Silas from the twins. Addie's "There they are!" was an echo of Ad's exclamation, and they flowed with the crowd down to the wharf, trying to keep Justin and Silas in sight, losing them in the press of people.

Addie was dizzy with excitement. It was like watching a dance. The crowd did nothing to interfere with the "Mohawks," who in turn carried out their mission as if they had long practiced it. Others joined the first group from various locations until there were three companies of "Native Americans" to row out to the tea ships, the *Dartmouth*, *Eleanor*, and *Beaver*, anchored in the harbor. Addie thought she saw Justin in one of the boats, but soon the motion obscured all.

"We must go home now. They will be hours at their work," Adrian said after they had watched over the water for long moments.

Addie resisted briefly, but then she allowed him to lead her away. There was no doubt about what the warriors were doing. Earlier in the day, John Rowe had asked the crowd, "Who knows how tea will mingle with salt water?" and a shout of approval had answered him. It would take time to dump the detested cargo into the sea.

"What if the soldiers come?" Addie asked, glancing around, struck by the realization that there were no redcoats in evidence but sure they would be very interested in this business.

"If they come, we don't want to be here." Ad tugged at her hand, hastening her along, but both of them were thinking about Justin and Silas, about what would happen if the soldiers caught them.

It was not the cold of the December night that made Addie shiver. Boston, indeed much of New England, had defied the government in various ways for years. The Stamp Act, passed in 1765, had caused such resistance and required so much effort and money in attempted enforcement that it had been swiftly repealed. The colonists would not tolerate having every official document, newspapers, and a host of other papers taxed with the required stamps. But in 1766, the same year as the repeal of the Stamp Act, a Declaratory Act had been passed to make clear that Parliament retained the right to tax the colonies. Soldiers had been quartered in Boston, and the tension between them and the civilian population had increased until it had culminated in what was known as the Boston Massacre because five civilians had been killed, three dying at the scene and two later as a result of their wounds. It was a measure of people's tempers that little note was made of the fact that the civilians had been armed with cudgels and the like and had been taunting the soldiers, nor was it often related that there may have been no clear order to fire. The soldiers had been withdrawn to Castle William, a fort on an island in the harbor, to ease the strain, but that was no real distance away.

What had gone before seemed in many ways worse than this night's work, but somehow, Addie knew it was not. She did not think so many people had ever gathered before in Boston or anywhere else in the colonies. And even now Justin, Silas, and other Sons of Liberty were deliberately destroying property in which the government had a vested interest. And Boston, surrounded by water with just a narrow neck of land connecting the city to the rest of Massachusetts, was vulnerable to control by forces of the Crown.

"Tonight, it is different, isn't it?" Her breath was a white plume in the darkness.

"Yes," Ad said, not needing her to explain.

Chapter 2

The twins finished the last part of their journey in a near run, trying not to stumble over refuse in the streets, though no soldiers, nor anyone else, impeded their progress. The soft glow of candlelight from their home had never seemed so welcoming.

The Valencourt house was nearly as fine as that of the Hancocks, which was acknowledged the best in Boston. Located in the South End on Summer Street, it was strong in brick, yet graceful in its symmetry and in the gardens around it. It was also large, a factor the twins hoped would help them now, as it often had in their comings and goings. They slipped around to the back, went in through the door to the winter kitchen, and found Tullia waiting for them.

She shook her head. "You two have the Devil's own luck. The mistress is having the baby, been working at it since early on. Your father has no idea you two have been gone nearly all day." Her frown deepened as she studied Addie. "You're sixteen years old, girl, you have no business running about in boy's clothes." But even as Tullia scolded, her hands were busy fixing plates of food for them.

No matter what mischief the twins got into, Tullia cosseted them. She had come north from Virginia with their mother, Lily Castleton. When Lily died, their father, Marcus Valencourt, had given Tullia her manumission papers. But Tullia had chosen to continue working for the Valencourts. She was head housekeeper and head cook, and all the servants in the household deferred to her or found themselves looking elsewhere for work. Tullia was patient with her underlings, and no one worked harder than she. Her rule brought order and harmony to Valencourt domestic affairs and, since their father prized these elements highly, the arrangement suited Marcus perfectly. It seemed to suit his current wife, too, for she had not sought to make any changes.

Marcus's first wife had been an Englishwoman. He had married Millicent Leighton in England before coming to the colonies with her in 1740. From that marriage he had two living children—Darius, who ran Valencourt business affairs in New York City, and Callista, who had reversed her parents' journey and lived in England with her English husband. Millicent had died of a fever in 1748.

Marcus had married Lily Castleton four years later, and from that marriage he had Justin, the twins, and their younger brother, Quentin. A son born after Justin and before the twins had died in his first year of life, and Lily herself had perished in childbirth four years after producing Quentin. The twins and Justin remembered Lily clearly, and Quentin thought he did because Marcus had encouraged their memories and had made sure they retained close ties to the Castletons in Virginia.

And now Marcus had a third family. He had married a widow, Mary Jenkins Tideman, the previous year. She had brought her two small children with her: Peter, who was five this year, and Jane, who was three. And she was laboring to present Marcus with another child.

Addie had been uneasy about her father marrying again, fearful of the upset that could bring. But her fears had proved unfounded. Mary was not one to make more work where things were running smoothly, and her energies were concentrated on loving Marcus, not on rearranging his household. At thirty-one, she was twenty-two years younger than Marcus, but that seemed to make no difference to her. Nor could her motive for marriage have been material gain as she had been left with a comfortable estate when her first husband died. And she was a comely woman, with dark-blond hair, soft features, and brown eyes. Soon after meeting her, Addie had understood why her father had seemed so much younger and happier. Now she was so fond of her stepmother, she didn't want to consider that they all might lose her in childbirth. She heard a muffled sound from the upper reaches of the house, and she shuddered.

"Two times before she has done this, and she says it went well. No reason for any trouble this time. She has the best midwife with her," Tullia said. Then her eyes narrowed as she looked from one twin to the other. "Something big happened out there, and you two were right in the middle. Justin, too. My Justin, he's all right? And Silas?"

They had never figured out how she did it. Her life seemed circumscribed by the house, yet she always seemed to know what was happening in the town, particularly when it involved any of "her" children.

They broke under her scrutiny, and the tale poured out, told in a two-voice chorus to the end.

"We know they went out to the ships."

"But we don't know what happened after that."

Tullia closed her eyes, mumbling to herself, then she drew a deep breath. "Those boys, they're lucky, too, they'll be fine. But you have to know this is no mere prank. This is serious. And it is going to break your papa's heart. He is the King's man, always will be."

"It is not the King who uses us so sorely," Ad protested. "It is Parliament and the King's Tory ministers." This was an old discussion for the twins, for they had gone over it often with Justin, and even with their father, who, for all his loyalty, thought the King was ill-advised and Parliament often blind regarding colonial affairs.

But Tullia did not share their view. "The King, he is the master. Doesn't matter what others do for him, he's the one who tells them or lets them do bad."

Addie knew it was futile to argue with her and, besides, it was too frightening to consider that she might be right. To defy Parliament and an assortment of ministers was one thing, to defy the King quite another—it was the road to treason and retribution.

They were saved from further discussion by their father's arrival. "Tullia! I have another… Oh, there you are!" He beamed at the twins. "Mary has given birth to a boy! We've named him Clement."

Marcus Valencourt was a tall, broad man, the strength of his frame belying his long years as a merchant and scholar. His dark hair was lightened with silver, but his dark eyes were bright with excitement over his new son and relief that his wife had survived the ordeal. He had seven living children. He named them in his mind: Darius in New York, Callista in England, Justin, Adrian, Ariadne, Quentin, and now

Clement. And though Mary's children were not his by blood, he loved them anyway. They made the total nine. He supposed he could add Silas to make ten, for Silas had been part of the family for years. He had had losses of children in both of his previous marriages, and Lily had been lost through childbirth. He knew how fortunate he was to have so many surviving children and a healthy, loving wife. He felt so content, he scarcely noticed that Addie was wearing her brother's clothes again, nor did he question how they'd spent their day. Instead, he urged them to come with him to meet their new brother.

Neither Addie nor Ad had the courage to mention to their father that Justin and Silas might be in dire trouble at this very moment. Though they, particularly Justin, were often at the family home, Silas had his own quarters in rooms above Valencourt's Book and Stationery Store, and for the past year, Justin had been living above Valencourt's Printing Office, next door to the bookstore on Cornhill, the main thoroughfare since the earliest days of the town. Tonight, the twins would just have to trust that the two had returned safely from the tea dumping.

The twins obediently admired Clement though, in truth, they shared the opinion that his red, wrinkled skin made him look like a miniature old man rather than someone newly born. Their next task was to placate Quentin, whose thirteen-year-old dignity was much injured by their having left him out of the adventure he was certain they'd had.

"You are always sneaking away without me," he complained.

"You wouldn't have liked it," Ad said. "We stood for hours listening to speeches."

Addie backed him up with a vigorous nod.

Quentin was mollified by this information, for he had no interest in speeches.

In the odd way of nature, Justin and the twins bore the look of Lily Castleton in their finely drawn features, golden brown hair, and eyes that Silas claimed made them look like fey wood spirits. But their minds were Marcus's legacy to them. They loved ideas for their own sake. They loved languages ancient and modern. Books were the most beloved of their possessions, and nothing was more enlivening than exchanging views about the contents of those books.

Quentin was cut of different cloth. He looked like Marcus, his hair and eyes dark, his features, even at his young age, reflecting the strong jut of brow, nose, and chin of his father. But he was no scholar. Most of what enthralled his siblings and his father bored him. Information and ideas were only interesting to him if they had some practical application. Justin teased that, to Quentin, the universe was nothing more than a machine.

Quentin's passion was for fixing things. Already he had proved useful with clocks, pocket watches, cooking spits—anything with parts that had to work together to work at all. To Addie, his mechanical abilities were marvelous alone, but his artistic talent astounded her. She could draw well enough, and she, Ad, and Justin could sing without disgracing themselves, but Quentin had been able to paint and draw with surprising skill before he could read and write, and he could play all sorts of musical instruments with little effort, as if the process of putting together images or musical notes required no more thought than breathing for him. These were Lily's gifts to Quentin. Marcus had saved scores of her drawings and watercolors, not dainty efforts but vivid proof of an artist's eye. And the older children could still remember the clear purity of Lily's voice singing to them.

Quentin adored Justin, so there was an added reason for the twins not to tell him what had transpired. It was a long night, especially for Ad, who shared a bedroom with Quentin. He couldn't sleep for worrying about Justin, and he wished he and Addie could have kept watch together.

With the dawn of the new day, all of Boston knew what had happened the night before. In less than three hours, the "Mohawks" had broken open and thrown into the sea three hundred and forty-two cases of tea. No damage had been done to the ships. Redcoats had never appeared nor had British guns fired. No one had been hurt, but great lumps of ruined East India Company tea were washing ashore.

Marcus was torn between joy at the birth of Clement and horror at what the "rabble" had done. When Justin arrived, having been summoned by messenger to greet his new half-brother, Marcus hardly gave him a chance to look at the new arrival before he demanded, "Do you know anything about this tea business?"

Justin met his father's eyes squarely. "No more than you, Papa, though I understand the reasons for it."

Justin loved and respected his father, and he winced inwardly every time he lied to him, but the truth would no longer serve. Justin was nineteen, but often these days he felt as if he were decades older. Keeping secrets from his family was a large part of the burden, but so was the terror of his thoughts about his duties and his rights as an Englishman. Though he had been only eleven years old during the protests against the Stamp Act, and though he had shared his father's horror at the unruly and destructive actions of the mobs that had gathered to protest and gone on to harass Stamp Act officials and destroy property, still there was inside of him an ever-growing conviction that the mother country and her colonies were drifting further apart than the broad expanse of sea that separated them.

It was not the same for his father. Though Marcus had prospered in America far more than he could have in England where, as a younger son of a family of moderate wealth and title, the best he could have hoped was to acquire a position in the clergy or a commission in the military, and though he had lived in America far longer than he had lived in England, he still considered himself entirely English. Despite living in Boston where the heritage of the Puritan founders was carried on by the Congregationalists, Marcus was an Anglican. He worshiped at King's Chapel, in the stone building that had replaced the wood of the first Anglican church in the Puritan town. It made sense to him that the King was head of the church as well as of the country, and he thought the Congregationalists and other extreme Protestant sects had much to answer for in what he saw as their encouragement of radical political views.

Marcus had returned to England only a few times since coming to America, but he referred to it as "going home," and when he received letters from relatives there, they were letters from "home."

Justin did not feel that way. He had spent a miserable year and a half at school in England. His father's people had been kind when he stayed with them at holidays, the studies had been easy for him, but he had been homesick not only for his family, but for his native land, and he had gotten in more than one fight when English-born students had mocked his accent and the colonies in general, calling the inhabitants rustics, provincials, criminals, and worse. Marcus had visited him, expecting to find the makings of an English gentleman, and had instead found a wild, too-slender young man who was more defiantly an American colonist than he had been on leaving Boston. When Marcus had sailed back to America, Justin had been with him. And Marcus had made no attempt to send Ad abroad. Ad had such a good grounding in the classics from Marcus and from tutors, and he was so bright, the year before, at fifteen, he had finished studies at the College of New Jersey at Princeton, a school favored by Virginian relatives and friends. Addie had hated having him away, but what Ad knew, she knew also, even if her access to formal education had been indirect, dependent on tutors who would allow her to listen to her brothers' lessons and on her brothers themselves and their willingness to share knowledge.

"Pardon?" Justin brought his wandering thoughts to the matter at hand. "I did not hear what you said."

Marcus's face reddened in frustration. "I said, what in the devil is this about? That tea those ruffians dumped in the harbor was to sell for less than one can buy it in England, for less than the price smuggled tea commands here. The duty of three pence per pound is the same as it has been for six years! Damn smugglers, New England is a nest of them! They don't want their illicit trade undermined."

Justin felt the sea widening between him and his father as it was between England and the colonies, but nonetheless, he felt obliged to reply. "The power of government lies in its treasury, in its power to tax to fill that treasury. The power of citizens lies in their having a voice in how they will be taxed and in how those taxes will be spent. You taught me this, taught me that the revolution in England less than a century ago was to make clear the voices of Englishmen in their government. King Charles I lost his head because he would not listen. But Parliament now treats us as if we were not Englishmen, as if we had no voice at all in the government. We are being taxed without being represented in Parliament."

"How could we be directly represented?" Marcus asked. "We would never have numbers enough in Parliament to vote our wishes and the distance is too far between here and England for such business to be carried out."

"There must be some way to balance affairs between the government and the colonies. There must! Else there will be more and more trouble. The Sugar Act, the Stamp Act, the Declaratory Act, the Townshend Acts, and the Tea Act, all of these and all the others, they will not serve!" Though he believed in what he was saying, Justin felt the futility of his words. The time for talking, for petitioning the King, for settling differences sensibly was slipping away. He had known that with every blow he had struck with his hatchet on the cases of tea. The low price of tea was perhaps the greatest insult, meant to tempt buyers to accept yet another constraint on trade in the form of a newly granted monopoly.

The East India Company was vital to Britain's financial empire, but the company had suffered heavy losses in supporting the war effort in India. To ameliorate these losses, the Company would establish warehouses in the main American cities, undersell American tea merchants, legitimate and otherwise, and monopolize the trade. By eliminating the intermediate agents and by taxing the tea at the old three-penny rate, the tea would be offered very cheaply, just as Marcus claimed. And from the government's point of view, the best part of the scheme was that the duty, no matter how small, continued to assert the government's right to tax the colonies without their consent. So the tea ships had come in spite of an attempt to ban British goods in general and tea in particular.

To Justin, this insult was as clear as a slap in the face, but he despaired of making his father perceive it that way. Marcus expected the government to wobble here and there because governments were never perfect, and he expected things to even out in the long run. Justin could not share his patience, but every time he met with other Sons of Liberty, every time he performed some service for them, and most of all last night on the tea ships, he saw his father's face, saw the pain and disappointment that would be there if Marcus knew what Justin and Silas had been doing.

The twins had shared a sigh of relief when Justin had come to the house, and Silas Bradwell with him, but they had been careful not to betray what they had seen. However, their efforts were in vain.

Giving Justin time alone with his father and the new baby, Silas visited with the twins. He had been part of their world since they were five years old, and they loved him as much as they loved their brothers. Though he hadn't done it much of late, when they were younger, he had called them "Ad-n-Addie" as if it were one word, teasing them because they planned most of their mischief together.

But this day there was no humor in his voice when he reverted to the nickname. "Ad-n-Addie, good day to you. It is a pleasure to see you both where you ought to be instead of where only two very foolish children would go. What did you think you were about last night?"

Ad looked abashed, but Addie's temper sparked. "We are hardly children. And surely you and Justin have more to explain about yesterday than we do. How do you think Papa would feel if he knew you are Sons of Liberty?" She was sorry the minute she said it; confirming to Silas that he and Justin had been seen with the "Mohawks", and that she and her twin knew they had not just been part of the crowd.

Suddenly Silas looked aged beyond his twenty-one years and so sad, Addie wanted to take back every word.

"I owe everything to your father. I honor him above all other men. But I cannot stand idly by while my rights as an Englishman are taken away. It was your father who taught me what those rights are. It grieves me that he and I are so far apart in this matter."

It was typical of Silas that he did not speak for Justin, only for himself, though he and Justin were in accord.

Addie couldn't bear causing him pain. "We won't tell. We've thought you and Justin were involved with the Sons of Liberty for some time now, and we haven't said anything."

"But you might avoid that nicked 'e' in the font if you plan to print any more broadsides," Ad offered. "Addie and I have noticed it several times. It helped make us suspicious. Of course, it's plain to us because I scarred it myself when I was trying to clean it with a knife once, but Papa might notice, too, because he caught me doing it. He was kind about it and turned it into a lesson about the proper way to clean type, but he dipped it in ink and printed it several times to show me what my knife had done. He probably remembers what that print looked like as well as I do. I don't think he ever forgets anything."

Silas shook his head as he studied them. "The two of you don't miss much, do you? But this isn't a game. The redcoats could have been called out yesterday."

"And then you and Justin might have been killed." Addie wasn't giving an inch. "We know it isn't a game. But we worry about both of you."

Ad wouldn't have said it in quite those words, but he agreed with the meaning.

"Justin and I are very careful, always," Silas insisted, but even as he said it, a tremor, part fear, part excitement, went through him, an echo of the previous day's events. He looked around at the rich furnishings and at the faces of the twins—Marcus's world, Marcus's children. When he was younger, Silas had dreamed of medieval knights and vows of honor, and in his secret heart he had imagined himself a squire to Marcus, prepared to swear his loyalty unto death. Now it seemed that for all he owed Marcus, for all he honored him, he and Justin were more likely to cause the man a broken heart than anything else.

Silas's father had died in the French and Indian War, fighting with the militia and redcoats against the French and their Indian allies. Silas, his mother, and two sisters had then lived on a farm with relatives, who had treated Silas's mother as an unpaid servant. When Silas was ten, his mother and sisters had died of smallpox. He had also been afflicted but had survived, as had most of the others at the farm, and when those relatives determined he wasn't going to die, they simply turned him out, deciding they had done quite enough for the little boy who showed no promise as a farmer. Silas hadn't begged to stay. He had walked to Boston, arriving ragged and hungry on the doorstep of Valencourt's Book and Stationery Store. The sheer gall of the slight, dirty child demanding to speak to Mr. Valencourt had so amused the clerk that he had told his employer, and Silas had met Marcus.

"I know how to read," Silas announced. "My mother taught me. She taught me numbers too. I want to work where there are many, many books." His mother had taught him to speak clearly as well, but she would not have approved of the belligerence in his voice.

Assuming he was a runaway, Marcus asked, "Does your mother or your father know you are here?" He had seen then the sheen of tears, there and quickly gone.

Silas tilted his head up and met Marcus's eyes. "My father was killed in the war when I was little. As for Mama, I don't know what she knows any more. She died some weeks back, and I am not certain whether she can still see me or not."

Marcus had known the truth of it even before he had gotten further details, and he had hired Silas on the spot, treating him as if he were a man rather than a lowly apprentice. And carefully, so as not to offend the boy's dignity, and with Lily and Tullia's help, he had given him the security of the Valencourt family, drawing him into their warmth as much as he could until it seemed as if Silas had always been with them, though he never consented to live in the Valencourt house.

Marcus considered himself amply rewarded for his kindness. Silas had learned bookselling, bookbinding, and the printer's art as well as any man, and through the years, though he had refused offers of formal education lest he be even more indebted to Marcus, he had read the "many, many books" of his dreams.

What Marcus did not fully comprehend was that Silas's mind had grown along with his body, until like old clothes, old ideas didn't fit either. Silas would give his life for Marcus Valencourt, but he would not give his obeisance to the tyranny of a parliament ruling from thousands of miles away.

The look of pain etched deep on Silas's face. It was an expression of raw grief, as if he were mourning the loss of something infinitely precious. It frightened Addie and made her want to take him in her arms and comfort him as if he were the younger one, not she.

"Really, I promise. Ad and I won't tell anyone," she said.

"I know you won't. But I want a bigger promise than that. I want you both to promise that you will never put yourselves in harm's way like that again." He spoke to the two of them, but it was Addie's eyes he held, looking at her in a way different from before, though she couldn't explain how.

"We'll try," Ad answered for them.

Although Addie wanted to offer more reassurance than that, she didn't. Like Ad, she didn't want to make a promise to Silas that they couldn't keep.

"Will you tell Justin you saw us?" she asked, knowing that her older brother would have cornered them immediately if he had known what they'd done.

"I'll try not to," Silas answered, a wry smile lightening the grimness in his face.

Justin was six feet tall, but Silas topped him by a couple of inches. Two years older than Justin, in many ways he had served as his older brother, as Justin was to the twins and Quentin. Darius, their half-brother from Marcus's first marriage, was thirty years old and had lived in New York for the past decade, too far away to be closely tied to his siblings.

After knowing Silas for so long, Addie had an odd, uncomfortable feeling that she was seeing him in a new way. With his dark hair and eyes, he looked as if he could be Marcus's blood son. But something about the way he had looked at her just now underscored the fact that he was not her brother. His lean face was harsh in its sculpture of strong bones, but his eyes were framed by long, thick lashes, and his mouth was beautifully shaped. His hands were long and lean like the rest of him, with calluses from his work with type and the printing press, but they, too, were beautiful, the fingers blunt-tipped, competent, yet graceful.

Addie felt the heat of a blush rising up her neck and coloring her cheeks as she wondered if he had kissed many women with that mouth, touched many of them with those hands. She was so shocked by her thoughts, she nearly gasped aloud. She had never had such thoughts before about *any* man and certainly not about Silas.

"Whatever is the matter with you?" Ad asked.

Addie's embarrassment increased until her checks felt as if they were afire. "My shoe pinches," she stammered and wished she could disappear through the floor as Ad and Silas exchanged grins, commenting without words on the foolishness of female complaints.

She was saved from further disaster by the reappearance of Justin.

"Papa wants to show off his new son to you," Justin told Silas, directing him to go upstairs. Then he turned to the twins. "So what do you think of our new brother?"

The abrupt return to normal concerns steadied Addie, and she let Ad answer for both of them. "I think he's not much to look at presently, but I expect he'll improve."

Justin laughed. "Honestly spoken, Brother, but I suggest you not tell his parents that."

Justin went on to speak of inconsequential things with the twins, and Addie kept up her end of the conversation, but all the while she was thinking of how changed everything was. She and Ad were keeping secrets from Justin, who thought he was keeping secrets from them, and all of them were keeping secrets from their father. Far from making her feel adult, it made her feel like a lonesome child. Curse Parliament! she thought. If the government would just relent, the troubles would cease before something worse than tea steeping in the harbor occurred.

Justin and Silas left the house together a short while later, promising they would be back for dinner on Sunday. As they walked along, Silas was thinking of what Ad had told him about the type on the broadsides and resolved to check for the "e" and any other distinctly marked pieces that might betray the clandestine printing they did for the Sons of Liberty.

Distracted, Justin's words took a moment to sink in, and even then, Silas couldn't credit them.

"What did you say?" Silas asked.

"I asked you when you were going to start courting Addie," Justin replied calmly.

Silas stopped dead. "Did you get hit on the head last night? Or is this because of Sarah Goodwin?" His attempt at levity was belied by his clenched fists and the tight effort in his voice.

Justin went on as if he hadn't noticed anything amiss. "Indeed, courting Mistress Goodwin has made me more aware of a lot of things, including the way you look at Addie. She's sixteen, you know, and though she still seems very young, she's going to grow up all of a sudden. You've loved her for a long time, and you've been patient waiting for her to grow up, but I hope you won't wait too long. I can't think of anyone who would make a better husband for her than you."

Justin felt quite pleased with himself. Everything he'd said was true, and he loved both Addie and Silas and thought they would suit each other well when the time came. He had been seeing things in a more romantic light since Sarah Goodwin had come into his life, but he had also seen how men were beginning to glance at his sister, at least when she was dressed as a female. She might not wish to grow up yet, but it was happening anyway, and he would like her to be in safe hands before he had to take action against those men who would look at her improperly, and before the political situation got any more dangerous.

He had thought Silas just needed a little encouragement. He was so stunned by the fury that contorted Silas's face, he took a step back.

"Don't you ever suggest such a thing again! Addie is a child, and even when she grows up, I would never presume to court her, never! After all your father has done for me, I would not so abuse him." He paused, drawing in a deep breath. "Ah, hell, Justin! I know you mean well. You honor me. But you are like my brother, she is like my sister, and it won't ever be more than that. I don't want to talk about it again."

Justin nodded, still shaken by Silas's anger, something he had rarely witnessed, but he also noted that Silas had not said he didn't love Addie. Justin wasn't sorry he'd broached the subject. Maybe it would make Silas change his mind over time.

They continued walking, and Silas tried to make Addie's image fade from his mind, but the harder he tried, the more vivid she became.

She looked like Adrian and Justin, and she looked entirely like herself. He knew how soft her hair would feel; when the dark brown and gold strands mixed it seemed to have its own light.

He wanted to trace the planes of her face, the straight nose and full mouth, the curve of cheekbone, slant of dark brows, and that determined chin. And her eyes, he could disappear into the gold that lightened the brown, disappear into the life and intelligence that shimmered there. The slightly almond shape of them fringed by dark lashes made her seem exotic even when he tried to remind himself that she was just the little girl he had known for so long.

But Justin was right. No matter how Silas tried to deny it to himself, Addie wasn't a little girl any longer. Justin was tall and slender, Ad was heading that way, and Addie had what Silas guessed would be her full height. She was tall for a woman, and he had watched her normal grace tangle in awkwardness sometimes when she was around women smaller than her. He wanted to tell her that her height for him was perfect, that her head would fit just so against the hollow of his neck, that he didn't mind if she stayed as slender as she was forever because there was something so essentially female about her, she didn't need lavish curves to prove it. He wanted to tell her a lot of things, lovers' nonsense and promises. He wanted to confess his dreams and share hers. He wanted a thousand things from her, and he wanted to give a thousand back.

He was ashamed of how he felt, of what he wanted, and he was determined she would never know about any of it. He was darkly relieved by his conviction that, given the way things were going in Massachusetts, soon there would be little time for romance.

Chapter 3

Williamsburg, Virginia

The government's retaliation for the tea dumping in Boston Harbor was harsh, yet it ignored the tea parties held in other colonies. On March 31, 1774, the Boston Port Act had been passed by Parliament, ordering that the port of Boston be closed on June 1, and remain so until the townspeople paid for the tea and proved they were loyal subjects. An offer to pay for the tea, but not the duty, met with no favor from the government.

The Boston Port Bill was just the beginning. Other coercive acts had been proposed and were, for a certainty, being passed in Parliament even now, though it would take time for confirmation to reach America. Each act was designed to humiliate, to punish, and to remind the colonies that power rested with Parliament in England. Lord North, First Lord of the Treasury, and thus Prime Minister and head of the government, was engineering the acts to isolate Boston as a warning to other cities and colonies that defiance of the government would not be tolerated.

It was clear that Lord North believed such treatment of Bostonians would prevent rebellion elsewhere. But if what the twins and Quentin witnessed in Virginia was any measure, Lord North was wrong.

Loyal Englishman though Marcus was, he did not want his children in danger and resolved to get them out of Boston until he could determine what changes to daily life the new government restraints would make.

His wife, Mary, baby Clement, and Mary's children, Peter and Jane, were packed off to the Tideman farm, some miles from Boston. Mary didn't want to leave Marcus, but she complied with his wishes. Had things been normal, she and the children would have spent time at the farm in the summer anyway. It was part of her first husband's estate and a place where she had spent happy times before. It was well-run by tenants who lived in outbuildings, not in the main house, an important consideration for Mary, who would not have wanted to put them out of their beds. The farm's orchards would be heavy with fruit in the summer, and there was bounty in the milk, cheese, and eggs produced in excess to sell in the towns. It was a good place for children, and that settled Mary's mind, as did Marcus's promise that he would spend as much time there as he could.

In early May, the twins and Quentin found themselves being shipped off willy-nilly to Virginia, and though Addie told Ad she thought their father was acting a good deal like Lord North himself, there was really no good excuse not to go. They had always enjoyed their time with the Castletons, and there was an added incentive this time because their Aunt Camille had been ailing during the past winter, and their Uncle Hartley had written to say how much she would like to see her niece and nephews now that she was feeling stronger.

Marcus wanted Justin to go with his siblings, but Justin would have none of it. "I mean to see that you do not lose what you have worked so hard to gain. With Boston being shut up like a prison, business is going to be very difficult. You will need Silas and me to help keep things going."

Marcus could not refute Justin's logic, and he was proud of both young men and recognized his need for them. He worried about Darius in New York, but that city was not Boston, and Darius had long since proved himself a capable merchant. Marcus would just have to trust him to carry on. Darius had been repaying his father's investment for some time, and before much longer the New York properties would be solely his.

Silas, no less than Justin, felt very guilty over the pride Marcus showed in both of them. It was not that they didn't intend to do the best they could for him, it was that they also intended to continue their work with the Sons of Liberty. The risks grew every day. But they would continue to gather information for the Committee of Correspondence that communicated with other such committees in the colonies; they would continue to print and distribute the broadsides that condemned Parliament's sins against Boston (Silas had made sure distinguishing type was no longer used for this); and they would continue to try to keep Marcus's newspaper, the *Boston Chronicle*, as toothless as possible.

Marcus no longer managed the paper day to day and left decisions more and more to Justin and Silas. Normally, the newspaper was innocuous enough, with its "poet's corner," local news, and parliamentary and court reports that were weeks out of date due to the sailing time it took to cross the Atlantic.

Before the Tea Party, Marcus had had the good sense to present political discussions in a balanced manner with the authors' names often concealed by noms de plume, though the noms de plume themselves were usually clear indications to the readers of the political loyalties of the writers. However, the destruction of property at the Tea Party had enraged and frightened Marcus. He wanted to blast the participants, using the pages of the *Chronicle* as weapons, but Justin and Silas had argued strenuously that the paper could lose much by railing too hard on either side of the issue. And in the end, it had been Marcus's love for balance that had convinced him as much as the arguments, and the paper's policy continued so in the face of the looming Coercive Acts.

Justin began to pity his father, something he had never expected because Marcus had always seemed so invincible to him. Though Marcus upheld the government's right to react to the Tea Party, the severity of the reactions made him uneasy.

"I think Lord North mistakes the temper of the colonies," he confessed to Justin. "What if this unites opposition rather than discourages it?"

"Then Lord North will have to reconsider his policy, won't he?" Justin replied, but he doubted that would be the case, the division between Tories and Whigs being so basic.

The Tories believed power should be vested in the Crown; the Whigs wanted royal authority limited, thus making Parliament more independent and less subject to the dictates of the King. Both sides were growing more unyielding by the day, and the Whigs, no matter how eloquent their pleas, voiced by such as Edmund Burke and William Pitt the Elder, for better treatment of the colonies, did not have enough votes or power to change the Tory government's course.

Justin eased the twins' sense of going into exile by asking a favor. "If it were possible, I would go with you. You know how much I love our Virginia relatives. But though I cannot go there now, you can observe firsthand how far Virginia is prepared to go to support Boston, if you would."

Addie liked the special purpose for the trip, but she also realized that she and Ad were being drawn further into the conspiracy against their father. No matter what his grievances against the government's policies, he would never countenance organized resistance to them.

It took Addie and her brothers two weeks to reach Virginia, allowing for a brief, rather formal visit in New York City with their half-brother Darius and his wife Harriet. The couple had been married for two years but, while Marcus had attended the wedding, for the twins and Quentin, this was their first meeting with Harriet. She was kind in her attentions toward them, although they had little time to get to know her. They traveled partway by ship and partway by carriage on bad roads, every mile of their journey planned by Marcus and arranged by agents he paid, and it would not do to disorder his careful schedule.

Because the General Assembly was in session, the family was in residence in Williamsburg, and the Valencourts received a warm welcome from their Aunt Catherine Lee Castleton—Uncle Hartley's wife—their cousin Sisley Anne, and Aunt Camille, Hartley's sister.

Aunt Catherine, a generously formed blond woman whose serenity provided a calm center for her family, immediately turned to the practicalities of making sure her nephews and niece knew which rooms were theirs, asking them whether they were hungry or thirsty, and generally seeing to it that they felt as if this was their home as much as hers. It was a ritual repeated every time they visited here or at the plantation.

Meanwhile, Sisley Anne, who was the same age as the twins, chattered away, trying to give her cousins all the news in a space of seconds. "Sissy" was blond like her mother but small and plump, and so quick moving and speaking it was hard to keep up with her. She hugged each of the Valencourts, her spate of words never faltering. "Hart is here with Papa, acting as his secretary, but Reeves is at Castleton. He's anxious to see you all, but it will have to wait until we go home. Oh, I'm so glad you're here. It's been too long!"

Addie was relieved to see that in spite of looking a little drawn, their Aunt Camille was obviously recovering from the illness that had threatened her during the winter, but still Addie hugged her so fervently, Camille laughed. "Child, you needn't worry. I am perfectly healthy now. We have had more cause to worry about all of you in Boston than you had to fret about me."

"Papa got us out of Boston before anything much happened," Ad offered, coming up to give Camille his own greeting.

"We didn't even get to see the soldiers who are supposed to come," Quentin said, aggrieved to have missed the splendid sight.

"Marcus showed good sense. A great mob of soldiers isn't a sight you need to see," Catherine told Quentin, and the sharpness in her voice was a revelation. She was usually soft-spoken and not given to voicing political opinions, despite her husband's long involvement in Virginia's government.

Camille bestowed a brief, tender look on her sister-in-law, and Addie thought of how well these two women shared the responsibilities for making her Uncle Hartley's life comfortable for him.

There had been four siblings in Hartley's branch of the family— Hartley, Lily, Camille, and Randal, but Randal had died in boyhood, and then Lily had died, so only Hartley and Camille were left, their parents having succumbed to fever within weeks of each other years ago.

Camille Castleton Stanhope had been married for a mere three years and had had no children when her husband was killed in a hunting accident. At thirty-seven, she had been widowed for more than a decade, but she showed no inclination to remarry, though suitors still came calling now and then. She had returned to her family home rather than live with her husband's people, but she did have a modest income from her husband's estate, which gave her a measure of independence. She was an integral part of Castleton, she and Catherine sharing the duties of the holdings with easy grace because while Camille liked the outdoor enterprises—the gardens, orchards, poultry—Catherine preferred to expend her energies on the household concerns of the plantation and the Williamsburg residence. Their efficiency left the men free to concentrate on the field crops, the horses, and such.

Aunt Camille was a favorite of all her nieces and nephews. She had been a tomboy in her youth and still loved to ride at faster than ladylike speed, regardless of the fact that her husband had broken his neck in a fall from his horse. She had encouraged Addie and Sissy to learn to ride, shoot, and swim as well as the boys. She believed that possessing a variety of mental and physical skills made a person, male or female, more interesting and healthier. Only recently had Addie realized that Aunt Catherine must have agreed with Aunt Camille since she had never tried to keep her children or the Valencourts from Camille's influence.

For the Valencourts, Aunt Camille was a special source of memory, too, for she and Lily had looked much alike, and the children felt as if their mother were somehow still with them when they were in Camille's company. She had the same touches of gold in her hair and eyes that the twins and Justin had gotten from Lily, and she gave Quentin his own image when she spoke of Lily's talent as an artist and musician. She had spoken to them often about their mother when they had come to visit as children, and some of the tales had been so frequently told, they knew them word for word. Addie's favorite began with, "Everyone was sure that when Lily visited England, she would be claimed by an Englishman, or perhaps by a fellow Virginian visiting there, but no one thought she'd fall in love with a man from Boston! But she did, oh my she did!" The story then went on in detail about the courtship of Lily and Marcus.

Camille kept track of family connections in the colonies and in England. No cousin, no matter how distant, went unrecognized, and in her fine hand, she sent letters hither and yon, keeping the various family branches tied together. Marcus teasingly called her letters "Camille's Chronicle," and said they came out more frequently than did his newspaper. But he had missed the letters this past winter, and worried about Camille as much as the children had.

In the afternoon, after dinner, Sissy took her cousins on a walk through the town, though it was more of an amble with many stops and starts, as Sissy was a friendly, popular young woman and knew a great many people. The Valencourts knew many, too, from previous visits, and when they stopped to talk, they were asked seemingly endless questions about conditions in Boston.

"It is all anyone talks about these days," Sissy told them. "I worry about Papa. He works too hard and is so troubled about how ill Parliament and the King's ministers are treating the colonies."

But in spite of the questions about Boston and Sissy's fretting, harsh politics seemed far away from this lush spring day. Winters here were much less severe and spring came sooner than in the North. Lilacs had already faded to give way to the color and scent of roses. There were flowers everywhere, and the wild birds seemed determined to sing until sundown with a bit of competition from domestic fowl and livestock wandering about. Even the human voices were different from those of New England, the Tidewater cadence softer.

Williamsburg was the capital, but it was also a small town with one major throughway, Duke of Gloucester Street, which ran from the College of William and Mary to the Capitol. The Castleton house, spacious and built of brick to endure, was off the Palace Green so that the Governor's Palace was to the right at the top of the green and Duke of Gloucester Street was to the left at the bottom.

Many of the larger homes were owned by families like the Castletons who lived in the country on their plantation but came into Williamsburg when the General Assembly was in session, usually in October and April, and accompanying social events were scheduled. The families with extensive landholdings were very much the aristocrats of Virginia, and they knew each other through many ties of kinship such as the Castletons had with the Lees through marriage.

Carriages trundled along Duke of Gloucester Street, and riders on horseback expertly controlled their mounts. There were farm wagons, too, pulled by humbler steeds, but most of the horses were finer than those in the North; sleek, powerfully muscled animals as showy as they were swift. People's clothing was also different, the fabrics lighter, so that the ladies seemed to float as they moved, and many men sported richer attire than sober Bostonians would approve. And though there were slaves, as Tullia had once been, in the North, there were far more here. There were some free Black people, but most were slaves, doing most of the work that kept everything running. Soft melodies drifted on the air, hummed or sung to the pace of the task as they worked.

Sissy spotted Richard Henry Lee in deep conversation with George Mason but would not have troubled them had not Richard Henry looked up as they passed.

His sober expression lightened. "Well met, cousins!" The Lee family with its multiple branches granted cousinage for the slightest connection by marriage. "It's been an age since Valencourts have ventured this far south. We must make sure you are so well entertained you will not wish to return to Boston."

Mr. Mason paid his respects, and then both men began to ask questions, as had others, about conditions in Boston.

Sissy shook her head as they finally walked on. "I vow, the only thing for it is to have Papa call a special session of the Assembly, then the three of you can tell everyone at once about Boston—" her voice broke off with a little yip of delight as she caught sight of her father and brother with another man.

Hartley Reeves Castleton was a tall, spare man in his early forties. The Castleton gold was bright in his brown eyes and in his hair. His broad smile came instantly at the sight of his daughter and the Valencourts, but the twins understood Sissy's worries. His face was more careworn than it had been the last time they'd seen him, and he was definitely thinner, as if the political wrangles were wearing at him.

With Hartley was his oldest son, Hartley Talbot Castleton, "Hart," who despite sharing a name with his father, had more the look of Catherine and Sissy, being blond and blue-eyed. The third man in the little group hung back a bit to allow the reunion, but he was well known to the Valencourts. Like Hartley, Richard Henry Lee, and George Mason, George Washington was a member of the House of

Burgesses and a planter with respectable holdings. Colonel Washington was also active in the militia.

His big frame topped six feet by enough to make Hartley and the rest of the gathering look short, and his rather solemn face added to the impact of his presence. But he was good-humored, his smile lighting his gray-blue eyes. After the family exchanges were done, he greeted the Valencourts warmly and said to Addie, "Mistress Valencourt, you have quite grown up since the last time I saw you."

Addie blushed, knowing from the gleam in his eyes that he was remembering that on that occasion she had been dressed in Ad's clothes, riding in a race against her cousins, Hart and Reeves. Hart winked at her, remembering, too.

Colonel Washington greeted Ad and Quentin with the same ease, but then he sobered. "You are so recently come from Boston, I would like to hear anything you can tell me about conditions and the temper there."

Sissy gave a little sigh of sympathy for her cousins.

"I would like to hear this as well," their uncle said, and he prevailed on the colonel to come home with them, which made the walk in the fading light even slower than before since now the young people were in the company of two prominent burgesses, and they were stopped often and questioned about how things were progressing in the Assembly.

The Assembly was a two-house legislature with the members of the House of Burgesses elected by citizens qualified to vote, while members of the Governor's Council were, like the governor himself, chosen by royal appointment. As they were chosen differently, so were they reacting differently to Boston's plight. The burgesses were showing increasing support for Boston, which in turn caused the governor and the council to plant their feet more firmly in favor of the home government's policies toward the colonies.

"Lord Dunmore would have liked not to call the Assembly into session at all," George said, "but there were matters to settle concerning western lands and the dispute with Pennsylvania over which colony has the legal claim. The governor had little choice but to have us meet."

Like their uncle and many other planters, Colonel Washington had a personal interest in those western lands in the form of financial investments and plans for future development.

"Both of you have been friends with Lord Dunmore for some time," Addie said. "It must be awkward now."

"Not really, at least not yet. Lord Dunmore is a consummate politician and loyal to the Crown, but it is not a personal affront to him that some should disagree. And in any case, he knows we, too, are loyal Englishmen," said Uncle Hartley.

For all his calm words, Addie had seen the swift look her uncle had exchanged with Colonel Washington, and she suspected there was something afoot of which the governor was ignorant. But she knew it would be useless to quiz either her uncle or the colonel; they were not men given to betraying political secrets.

At the Castleton house, after pleasantries were exchanged with the women, and Hart and Sissy took Quentin off to entertain him, the men questioned the twins at length and were so attentive, Ad and Addie worked hard at remembering even the smallest details of broadsides they'd read, conversations they'd overheard, everything except the fact that Justin and Silas were members of the Sons of Liberty. They omitted that by unspoken consent because it was not their secret to share.

"What of your father? How is he weathering all of this?" their uncle asked.

"It is difficult for him," Ad said. "You know how he is. He likes things to go smoothly in business, in politics, in everything. It worries him that all is so unsettled now. Most of all, he fears what will happen when soldiers are again quartered in the town. That's much different from having them at Castle William in the harbor and in small numbers."

"Indeed, it is," Colonel Washington agreed. "Soldiers and civilians are seldom a peaceful combination." He spoke from experience having fought, as had Hartley, in the French and Indian War. During that conflict, Washington had visited Boston, and so he was more familiar with New England than most Virginians.

As though in a deliberate effort to avoid any more talk of political tensions, the conversation turned to the land. Hartley and George were well matched in many ways. They were both in their early forties and both typical of the Virginia gentry. They enjoyed horse racing, card playing, dancing, and theatrical performances, all pastimes condemned in Massachusetts. Most importantly, they shared a passion for the land and were determined to use the newest methods of crop rotation, fertilizers, and the like to repair the damage heavy-feeding tobacco did to the soil.

But even farm concerns came back to politics.

"Tobacco ties us too closely to England. It must be transported in English ships and sold by English merchants, and, too often, there is damage in transit, or a claim that less has arrived there than we sent," George said. "Or they sell it for too little, and the finished goods we order from them are overpriced and of poor quality."

"But George has made great strides in breaking the cycle, and I have also, following his lead," Hartley said. "New Englanders are far ahead of us in having their own manufactories to supply finished goods to local markets, no matter how much the government has tried to discourage them. Unlike those colonies, we haven't many towns of any size, so it is difficult—each plantation must be its own small town—but it can be done. Like George, we're producing more wheat and milling it ourselves. We're making our own cloth, not the fine stuff of ball gowns, but good, strong workaday cloth. And though our attempt at a fishery hasn't been as successful as his, still we're able to send some fish along with wheat and flour to the West Indies where we can get foreign goods or money for them. It's a much better arrangement than blindly sending tobacco to England and trusting the best will be done for us."

The twins knew that the colonel deserved the credit their uncle gave him. He had not had the indulgent education offered to many planters' sons—his father had had financial difficulties, and George had not been the oldest son anyway—but his talent for mathematics had gotten him good jobs as a surveyor from a young age. Then his marriage to a wealthy widow, Martha Danbridge Custis, in 1759, had vastly improved his fortunes, as had becoming the proprietor of

Mount Vernon, the estate once owned by his half-brother Lawrence who had died in 1752. He had paid rent to Lawrence's widow for ten years, but after her death, Mount Vernon became his.

He had a charming way with women, but few doubted his devotion to Martha or his kindness to the two children—John, "Jacky," and Martha, "Patsy"—she had brought to the marriage. Addie hated to interject a sad note, but she felt the omission would be uncivil.

"Aunt Camille wrote to us about Patsy's death last year. We were sorry to hear of it."

For a moment, grief was stark on his face at the mention of his stepdaughter. "It was a terrible loss for her mother and me. We appreciated the letters of condolence sent by your family."

His mood brightened. "But now we have something to celebrate. I can hardly credit that Jacky has just married Mistress Nelly Calvert of Maryland. She is a great comfort to my wife. I confess, I'd thought Jacky a bit young and unsettled for matrimony—he's only twenty, after all—but perhaps Mistress Nelly will settle him. Mayhap, Mistress Addie, we will find a Virginia beau for you. It would be simple justice since your father carried your mother away to New England."

Unbidden, Silas's image came to her mind, as clearly as if he were standing beside her, and she was so startled, she barely restrained a cry of surprise. "I think my father might not agree with you," was all she could manage.

The colonel had the grace to let the subject drop.

They shared a light, late supper before Washington departed, and by the time the household settled down for the night, all three Valencourts were so tired from the long journey south and from the excitement of the day, they fell asleep as easily as if they were in their own beds, Ad and Quentin sharing a room and Addie sharing with Sissy. But as exhausted as she was, Addie still had energy enough to dream of Silas.

She dreamed he had come to Virginia and that they danced together at a party at Castleton. They walked in the gardens and she was dressed in a silk gown that shimmered in the moonlight.

She dreamed until she heard Sissy urging, "Wake up, sleepyhead! It's ever so late! And did you know you were calling to Silas? Of course he is the Silas in Boston, but I thought he was like a brother. I wish you had a miniature of him. I'd like to see what he looks like. Is he very handsome? Does he know how you feel? Does he feel the same?"

Addie blinked at her, trying to gather her wits against the rapid flow of words from her cousin, who had obviously been up for hours. "I don't know what in the world you're talking about," she lied when Sissy finally started to wind down. "If I called Silas's name, it must be because I am worried about him and Justin. I don't want them to get into trouble with the redcoats."

Sissy studied her, a little frown marring her forehead. "Well, you didn't sound worried. You sounded… I don't know, soft, not like you usually sound."

"Thank you very much! I suppose I usually sound like a harridan?" Addie teased in mock anger, but Sissy had already flown to the next subject, her own secret. "I'm in love with James Fitzjohn, but he seems to have eyes only for Cordelia Wakefield."

"Does he still call you 'brat'?" Addie asked with a smile, but it occurred to her that Sissy's case was very similar to her own, for James Fitzjohn was a friend of Sissy's brothers and had always treated Sissy as a little sister.

"Yes, but in a different way. I'm not sure. Oh, bother! It's hard to explain, but I'm going to bring him to his senses just as soon as I figure out a plan."

Addie laughed aloud at that. "Sissy, your plans are apt to get you into difficulties. Do think before you act." She doubted her warning would do any good; Sissy often behaved as impulsively as she talked.

In another shift of subject, Sissy said, "We must go through your clothes. Mama will fuss and fuss unless we've already got a good idea of what you'll need."

Addie made no attempt to stop Sissy from plowing through her belongings. This was part of the ritual of a visit to Virginia. Marcus was generous in the matter of his offspring's wardrobes, but not only was the climate in Virginia different, so was the social life, and Aunt Catherine enjoyed having another girl to dress. Further, the last time Addie had been here, she had been fifteen. Two years shouldn't make such a difference, but they would. She was certain both of her aunts would expect her to dress much more elaborately than she had before, just as there was a new, more mature look to Sissy's clothing than there had been. Addie could only hope that she would be allowed more informal wear at Castleton.

It seemed as if she were going to grow up whether she wished to or not, and she suspected sending her to Virginia at this time must have seemed doubly fortuitous to her father. He would trust her aunts to take her in hand in the gentlest way, a role that would be difficult for his wife Mary and for Tullia. Though he wouldn't say it, he thought Tullia was too indulgent with Lily's children, and he knew himself to be likewise guilty.

Addie didn't want to disappoint her aunts, but she imagined they were going to discover that making her into a proper young woman was going to be no easy task. She was taller than most women, and she didn't have a fraction of the curves Sissy had. It seemed to her a matter of trying to make a silk purse from a sow's ear.

Then, before she could stop herself, she wondered if Silas would notice her in a new way if she changed, and if he would approve. In the next instant, she was chiding herself and resolving not to think of Silas any more. She wondered if part of growing up was to be embarrassed by one's own thoughts. If so, she hoped it wasn't a frequent occurrence.

For the next few days, she saw little of Quentin, who was finding all sorts of things to sketch and investigate, and even less of Ad. He was off with Uncle Hartley and Cousin Hart and fascinated with the workings of the Assembly. Addie wished she could be with him, but she resigned herself to choosing fabric—muslin, gauze, lawn, linen, silk, lace plain, patterned in the weave, printed, embroidered, so many colors and patterns that Addie soon grew confused by the choices and left it up to Aunt Catherine—and to fittings with the mantua-maker tutting that though Mistress Ariadne had few curves, neither did she need tightly laced corsets. Addie let it all pass without comment; she couldn't do anything about her shape, and she wasn't much worried because Aunt Camille didn't approve of tight lacing, particularly in the young, so Addie knew she was safe from that torture.

She told herself any sane young woman would enjoy all the fuss and finery, but she felt guilty. It wasn't the expense, because she knew the cost of all the garments and accessories together would mean little against the Castleton wealth. It was the politics involved. Politics were everywhere, it seemed, even in choosing a dress. While Uncle Hartley and Colonel Washington might be encouraging cloth manufacture on their plantations, these fabrics she would be wearing were all imported, some from as far away as China and India, sold by English merchants and carried in English ships. They were clear proof that attempts to avoid English goods hadn't been successful, and they reminded her of how dependent Virginia was on trade with England and of how that must influence how much or how little the burgesses would support Boston.

She traced the intricate embroidered flowers on a piece of cream silk, hardly hearing Sissy and Catherine discussing what colors were best for her while Camille looked on, thinking instead that such fabrics as this beneath her hand would soon be unobtainable in Boston save for those the merchants still had in stock. With the port closed, it was not only fine fabrics that would be in short supply. She shivered in the warm air. Boston was so easy to isolate.

Camille's voice was soft. "For all the grown-up clothes, you are so young. Enjoy it while you can. I know your thoughts, and you are right. But if things go as they are, we will all be wearing homespun soon enough. You cannot change what will come by mourning over this cloth or any of it. It's all very confusing, isn't it?" Her look was infinitely tender, and for a moment, Addie imagined it was her mother Lily speaking, and she was comforted.

Later when Ad returned to the house, Addie cornered him, demanding information. "I am being extraordinarily patient with being decked out like a mantua-maker's doll while you spend little time with the tailor for your new feathers. I would much rather be with you and Uncle Hartley. Can you tell me what is going on in the House of Burgesses? It's something very important. I can feel it! You, Uncle Hartley, and Hart are all behaving as if you are keeping a very big secret."

Ad struggled only briefly with his conscience. He and Addie had always shared everything, and he was accustomed to having her ideas to compare with his. It was a relief to tell her. "The House is going to declare for Boston, and the burgesses know that when they do that, Lord Dunmore will dissolve the Assembly."

They were both silent for a long moment, and then Addie said, "It is the best that Justin and Silas could hope for. And it is the worst for Papa. If two colonies so different from each other can act together in defiance of the government, then surely others can do the same."

"They will," Ad said, absolute conviction in his words.

But neither of them could imagine where such a course would lead with stubbornness on both sides growing more entrenched.

Just as Ad had said, on May 24, the House of Burgesses approved a measure that set aside the first day of June for fasting, humiliation, and prayer in Virginia. They had waited until late in May to keep the Assembly in session as close to the June 1 date as they could, June 1 being the date dictated by the government to close the port of Boston.

The governor dissolved the Assembly on May 26, but rather than dispersing, the burgesses adjourned to the Apollo Room in the Raleigh Tavern and continued their discussions about how to encourage colonial unity.

Ad was dazzled by the sure purpose of his uncle and the other men, and he listened as the radicals, including the fiery-tongued Patrick Henry, George Mason, Richard Henry Lee, and others, argued to forbid exports to Britain as well as imports, while the moderates, among them Uncle Hartley, Peyton Randolph, Carter Braxton, and a delegation of local merchants, argued that it would be self-destructive to forbid the exports on which they were so dependent.

These Virginians had always seemed larger than life to Ad, many of them physically imposing, tall, strong men, and many descended, as the Castletons were, from Loyalists from the court of Charles I, cavaliers who had emigrated to Virginia in the decades after Virginia had been made a royal colony in 1624. Their ideas were as grand in stature. Radical or moderate, they were Englishmen determined to be fairly treated by their government. They might differ on how this was to be achieved, but they were all loyal to the King and sure that he would heed their petitions of plea and protest if only his ministers and Parliament did not misdirect him. After all, King George III was English born, unlike his grandfather, George II, whom he had succeeded. In his maiden speech when he had become King in 1760 at the age of twenty-two, he had declared, "Born and educated in this country, I glory in the name of Britain." And his exemplary home life with Queen Charlotte had come as a relief to many of his subjects after the dissolute lives of the first two Hanoverian kings. And yet, his blood was not English, Welsh, or Scottish. He was king only as a result of Britain's torturous efforts to escape the return of Roman Catholic dominance and the belief in the absolute rights of monarchs the royal line of Stuarts had proven incapable of relinquishing.

"The King enjoys the simple pleasures of country life, so he must understand the passion and concerns of his farmer subjects, mustn't he?" Ad said, finishing his recital to Addie of what he'd observed and heard among the burgesses.

"Maybe not," Addie replied. "After all, being a king and dabbling now and again in the fresh air is hardly the same as being dependent on the bounty of your own fields. What if Tullia is right? What if the King is the master after all? What if he has not been misled by his ministers but has himself deliberately directed the harsh measures against the colonies? What then?"

Ad contemplated this, but then he shook his head. "It cannot be so! It cannot! If the King is so against us, then we are lost. And even the little justice we ask might be seen as treason."

"We ask." The phrase rang in Addie's head. She acknowledged that she was part of it as Ad was, more a part of it every day, as were Justin and Silas and many more. As was Uncle Hartley despite his stand with the moderates. As their father would never be. A sudden wave of homesickness for him washed over her, and Ad squeezed her hand in understanding and reassurance.

"I think Papa believed he was sending us away from strife," Ad said, his voice unsteady. "He doesn't want to see how far things have gone not only in Boston, but here and everywhere throughout the land.

There is talk of representatives from all the colonies meeting together soon, not just writing to each other, but meeting face to face."

They didn't say it aloud to each other; they didn't need to. They both knew that such a meeting, unsanctioned by the government, would be the most daring action taken so far by the colonies in their struggle with Parliament and the King's ministers—and perhaps with the King himself.

The first of June was everything the burgesses had hoped it would be. Peyton Randolph, Speaker of the House of Burgesses, led the procession down Duke of Gloucester Street, and prayers for the people of Boston were offered in the churches.

Addie offered her prayers for her father, for Justin, for Silas, for all of them, and for the men of the government in England that their hearts might soften and their minds open.

Strangely, Uncle Hartley and Colonel Washington continued to dine with the governor, their relationship as cordial as ever.

"Lord Dunmore seems to believe the high temper will pass and affairs will return to normal." Uncle Hartley sighed heavily. "I wish I could share his optimism." Then his face brightened. "But at least, now we can go home to Castleton."

"I'll wager ol' Reeves has missed us!" Hart said.

"As we have missed him," his mother said, adding, "I expect the house will celebrate our return, too."

"And the gardens!" Aunt Camille's eyes sparkled in anticipation of returning to her beloved herb and flower beds.

Addie was sure Sissy's flush of excitement had to do with the prospect of seeing James Fitzjohn again rather than her brother Reeves, the house, or gardens, but it didn't matter. Castleton meant something special to each of them, and its magic was awaiting them.

Chapter 4

Castleton Plantation, Virginia

They traveled by boat up the James River, arriving at Castleton's wharf on a warm afternoon. Warehouses and boathouses along the shore told of how important the tidal river was to the commerce of the plantation. The people of Castleton were gathered to welcome the master and mistress home, and over the whole busy scene rose the main house, three storys of red brick with a steeply sloped roof and tall chimneys in pairs at both ends. It had been placed on a gentle slope above the river to command a magnificent water view from the front and the prospect of gardens and fields from the back. There was a two-story wing on each side of the central building, and though the wings were not connected to the house, they complemented the style.

The house had been completed only forty years before, but the land had been claimed by Castletons for nearly a hundred and thirty years. There were major branches of the family in England and minor branches scattered across Maryland and Virginia, but in the colonies, this was the family seat. And everything about it reflected balance, grace, and wealth. Even the dependencies—the smoke, bakery, and spring houses, the mill, stables, workshops, greenhouses, and everything else needed for the running of what was really a village—had been constructed with an eye to fitting into the whole. The aristocracy of Virginia—the Carters, Byrds, Harrisons, Lees, Washingtons, and others—felt as at home here as they did on their own plantations.

Reeves strode forward, unreserved in his pleasure at having his family home again. Reeves Lee Castleton was the image of his father and thus looked as if he were more closely related to the twins than to his siblings. He greeted them all exuberantly, hugging Sissy with one arm and Addie with the other after he had greeted his elders.

"Reckon you girls are in for some spoiling this summer. Addie, Hart and I will spoil you, and Ad and Quentin can spoil Sissy."

"More likely there'll be twice as much teasing," Sissy said, but she reached up to give him a smacking kiss on the cheek.

Hartley immediately wanted to know how things had gone at Castleton in his absence, and Reeves was proud to report that all was flourishing.

"You might have mentioned at least one disaster in order to assure me that I am needed here," Hartley said. "Failing that, I will have to resign myself to having a son who is becoming a better farmer than I. You have my thanks for your good work."

In truth, though Addie knew Reeves to be just as competent as his father claimed, she could not imagine life at Castleton running any way but smoothly. Even the children had jobs to do, whether it was picking fruit and vegetables or stirring the air and keeping the insects away as their owners and guests dined or gathered to converse.

Addie, with her siblings and cousins, spent as much time as she could riding, fishing, and rambling the countryside. Quentin was the exception; he spent his time producing piles of sketches or inventing new musical rhythms that hummed in his head and on his recorder.

"That must be perfect bliss," Addie whispered to her brother when they came upon Quentin making music one evening. Quentin's face was radiant as the notes rose and fell in ancient harmony.

Ad nodded. " Quentin would be the happiest man alive if he could do this for the rest of his days. What if every man on earth has been born with the right to determine his own life?"

"What if every woman has been born with that same right?" Addie's voice was tart.

"I think that might be taking the argument too far," Ad said and received a sharp jab in the ribs.

"Pray remember that I've always shared my books and tutors with you," he protested self-righteously, but then he had the grace to add, "though I'm forced to admit you've always been as good a student as I."

"Better."

"I surrender. Better it is."

Ad was surprised when his sister hugged him, and he heard the quaver in her voice. "I wish I could share it *all* with you! I know you and Hart and Reeves have been practicing cavalry drills. I heard you talking, and I followed you when you said I couldn't come with you."

She could see them clearly in her mind's eye. Their swords had been fashioned of wood, weighed at the point to give the heft of a blade and to strengthen their arms, but it hadn't been like boys playing. They had ridden down their stuffed targets and slashed with deadly purpose.

"Addie! As game as you are, there are things you just can't do! And being a soldier is one of them."

She knew he was right, but that only made her angry. "I would rather be a soldier than wait to hear that my brothers and cousins and... their friends"—she barely prevented herself from saying Silas's name—"have been shot or hacked to pieces by the redcoats."

Besides their secret association with the Sons of Liberty, Silas and Justin openly belonged to the prestigious Boston Grenadier Corps, a militia unit that required, among other things, that all of its members be five feet ten inches or taller. In the past, muster days had been boisterous celebrations with the men parading proudly in their uniforms and then enjoying generous amounts of liquor so that the whole endeavor resembled a fair more than a military exercise.

Addie feared those light-hearted muster days were gone forever. Despite their disdain for the citizen-soldiers, Crown authorities had of late eyed the militia with suspicion, trying to limit their access to military stores beyond the arms the men provided themselves.

The notes of Quentin's recorder rose high and hauntingly sweet.

"There is little chance of a battle," Ad assured her. "You know as well as I that every effort is being made to prevent bloodshed."

"I wish I could believe that." She turned on her heel and left. She couldn't stand to hear another word. In the alchemy of her mind, the wooden swords were transmuted into shining, knife-edged metal.

Ad watched her go. He felt the beat of war, too, and despite his apprehension, a frisson of excitement ran through him. He could feel the horse thundering beneath him, could feel the weight of a finely wrought sword. But then looking at Quentin in the fading light, he saw their father in the dark hair and eyes, and the battle fire died as abruptly as it had ignited, leaving him cold and empty.

In July, the Castletons hosted a party that began with a lavish picnic in the afternoon and went on through most of the night with music and dancing. Many people came many miles and were given accommodations at the plantation. Lee cousins came from a good distance, from Lee Hall, Stratford Hall, and even from Leesylvania; Byrds arrived from nearby Westover; Harrisons from Berkeley; Carters from Shirley Plantation; Littlefields, Chamberlaynes, Bassetts, and Custises, on and on—they came until Castleton was overflowing with people of all ages.

Sissy was beside herself, fluttering about like a demented butterfly because James Fitzjohn had arrived. She had watched from an upstairs window until she saw him, and then she nearly yanked Addie's arm out of the socket dragging her over to look.

"Isn't he the most handsome man you've ever seen?"

James Fitzjohn was of medium height, solidly built, with muscular horseman's legs. Addie remembered his good humor and his easy smile. His dark-brown hair and eyes were a perfect foil for Sissy's blondness. But Addie couldn't resist teasing, "I suppose he is presentable."

Sissy hardly heard her as she continued to gaze down at her beloved. Then she stiffened as she caught sight of another guest. "Oh, fie! There's Cordelia Wakefield. I hoped she wouldn't come. She's dressed as if the dancing is beginning already. Maybe I ought to change my dress, maybe…"

"Maybe you ought to just be yourself," Addie suggested gently. "Cordelia is over-dressed for a picnic. There's no sense in you following her lead. You look fetching just as you are."

Sissy's gown was pale blue with darker blue patterning the underskirt. The front of the gown was fitted and not too low cut, the back an easy fall of two long pleats. The cotton cloth was from India, and the gown was cool and appropriate for the festivities and her youth. It brought out the blue of her eyes, and she was very pretty in it. But Addie had to admit to herself that that might not be enough to dazzle

Mr. Fitzjohn in the face of Cordelia's splendor. Cordelia had blue eyes, too, but her hair was jet black, her skin cream and roses. She was a bit shorter than her escort and well shaped. Today she was clad in heavy rose silk, and her hair was piled high with a ribboned hat tipped forward on it, as if she were going for a promenade in a London park instead of spending a day out in the countryside of Virginia.

Addie was dressed much like her cousin, though her gown was done in shades of forest green. She would have preferred to have been wearing Ad's clothes and wished she could compete in the races that would soon be run, but with an inward sigh she conceded the impossibility of that at her age. So far, growing older didn't seem to be much fun.

"Come on, Sissy, put on your hat. You might as well make your entrance, Cordelia or not."

Unlike Cordelia's, the hats the cousins wore were practical rather than fashionable, wide-brimmed to shade their faces.

Outside they were immediately enveloped in the noise and color of the day as people moved about visiting and eating from the vast array of dishes set out on plank tables under the trees above the river. It might have been a picnic, but the tables were covered with linen, silver, and fine porcelain. And the bounty of Castleton was offered in ham, chicken, beef, and fish, fresh fruits and vegetables, baskets of biscuits and bread offered with crocks of fresh butter and honey, and sweet cakes, all of it accompanied by beverages from as mild as cold spring water to fruit punches to Madeira and the most potent rum.

Addie quickly began to reconsider the prospect of growing up. Perhaps it wasn't such a bad thing after all. She and Sissy were immediately surrounded by young gentlemen who begged to be allowed to bring a bite of this or a drink of that to the ladies. It was a bit foolish, but it was also enjoyable. She felt a sense of power she'd never known before. Then she glanced over and saw her twin rolling his eyes at her, and she nearly laughed aloud.

She wasn't aware of Sissy's determined pursuit of her quarry until they were face to face with James Fitzjohn and Cordelia Wakefield.

"Hello, Brat," James said, but Addie saw the way his eyes lighted and understood what Sissy had been saying.

However, Sissy seemed to have lost her confidence in the presence of Cordelia, and Addie could almost feel her wilt beside her. Still, Sissy went on gamely. "You remember my cousin, Ariadne Valencourt?"

Both James and Cordelia allowed as how they did, but then James said, "Mistress Valencourt, I swear I didn't realize that New England creates women every bit as lovely as Virginia does."

It was a commonplace enough compliment but not under the circumstances, and Addie wanted to kick James in the shins for it. Worse, Cordelia, who was as good-natured as she was beautiful, smiled pleasantly at both girls, showing no signs of jealousy in spite of the fact that Sissy was gazing at James as if he were a Greek god.

"Sissy, I want to see the horses before the races begin," Addie said. "Shall we go see what kind of odds there will be against our brothers?" She clamped her fingers so firmly on Sissy's arm, her cousin had little choice in the matter, and when she started to sputter a protest, Addie gave her a little jerk to set her in motion.

Behind them, they heard Cordelia explaining that she didn't really want to see the races, all the dirt and heat, don't you know? Addie suspected James had been ready to accompany them to the event.

"What does James find so perfect about her?" Sissy fumed when they were out of earshot.

"I'm not sure he finds her perfect. He looked a little bored," Addie said, hoping she was right as Sissy brightened at the thought.

Just in time, they got to the area where the racecourse had been set out. The horses were prancing nervously under the weight of their gentlemen jockeys, and Addie felt a thrill of pride as if she were Virginia born. There were no better horses or horsemen in the colonies than those of Virginia. The big, blooded horses and their riders were a noble sight.

Though she envied Ad, she was proud of him. He was astride a five-year-old thoroughbred chestnut stallion from the Castleton stables, and he looked as much at home in the saddle as anyone there.

Sissy looked at her brothers and cousin. "Maybe with three Castleton entries, we have a chance against Harry Lee. He rides like a demon."

The young men were competing in two-mile heat races, the winner to be the first one to take two heats. Sissy and Addie cheered wildly for their brothers, and the trio upheld Castleton honor, riding neck-and-neck with the leader. But the leader was unbeatable. Just as Sissy said, Harry Lee rode like a demon, and he didn't even have to compete in a third heat, having won the first two by a clear margin.

Henry, 'Harry' to all who knew him, was one of the Lees of Leesylvania, a cousin to the Stratford Lees and to the Castletons. Like Ad, Hart, and Reeves, he had attended the College of New Jersey at Princeton. He had graduated the previous year, and now, at eighteen, he was not sure what he would do. There had been some talk of him going to England to study law, but with the political trouble between Virginia and the mother country, that oft-followed course no longer seemed so sensible, particularly since he numbered among his relatives such as his cousin, the radical Richard Henry Lee. Though slightly built, Harry was a comely young man as quick-witted as he was athletic, and he was so well liked that Ad, Hart, and Reeves congratulated him heartily for beating them.

"Truth to tell, the horses decided it among themselves while we just sat there," Harry said with a grin.

They stayed to watch other races, but Hart noticed that Sissy kept casting longing looks back toward the house. "No luck today?" he asked softly. "James still blind?"

Sissy flushed with embarrassment. "How did you know? Oh, never mind! I know I follow him around like a pitiful pup. And he's not blind at all, not when it comes to Cordelia Wakefield. Lately I've even thought he's seen the changes in me, but I guess they're pretty hard to notice when Cordelia's about."

"Pitiful pup. Well, I don't think it's quite that bad. But James does seem blind where you're concerned, as you are about the interest other men have been showing in you lately." He smiled and nodded at her disbelief. "It's true. I've been watching them very carefully. It won't do to have just any suitor begging for my little sister's hand. James is a good man, and he deserves better than Cordelia. She's the kind of woman who is as happy with a mirror as with a man. And I don't think she's serious about James, nor he about her, come to that." He paused, studying his sister's face under the shade of her hat. "Are you? You are only seventeen. I want what's best for you, but I don't want James to have his heart broken."

He could see how amazed she was at the idea she could do anything at all to James Fitzjohn's heart.

"I won't break his heart. I will take very, very good care of it if I ever have the chance." She spoke as if taking a vow.

For all the older-brother teasing Hart had engaged in over the years, he loved his sister, and he knew her well, perhaps better than she knew herself. She was as lively and chattery as a wren, but she was also funny, kind, and intelligent. And though she might seem carefree on the surface, she was steadfast; her loyalty and love did not change. She had loved James for a good while; it was time for him to see her in a new light.

"You won't say anything to him?" she asked anxiously, as if reading Hart's mind.

"I won't betray your trust," he promised, and Sissy had to be content with that. He didn't want to admit it even to himself, but with the way things were going in the colonies, he felt a sense of urgency about his sister, a need to have her settled and happy as soon as possible with the man she had chosen. It would not have surprised him to know that his cousin Justin had similar thoughts regarding Addie, for everyone seemed to be considering things more carefully these days. Golden interludes like this one at Castleton suddenly seemed infinitely precious and fragile. If relations with the government continued to deteriorate, who could foretell how changed life would be, especially in Virginia, a colony so dependent on trade with Britain. Hart began to rehearse the role he would play with James.

Lanterns were hung on the trees outside and lined the paths as evening fell, and inside the rooms glowed with candlelight reflected on the shining floors, on the polished surfaces of furniture, and on the mirrors that made the walls on which they hung seem insubstantial and expanded the boundaries of the rooms.

Addie's thick hair was piled high on her head and wound with a few fresh blossoms from Camille's gardens. Her dress was made of the cream silk embroidered with flowers. It was fitted to the waist, but the skirt was full, given shape by hoops. The sleeves were tight to just above the elbows where three deep, sheer ruffles cascaded to her wrists. The slightest movement of her hands or arms caused the ruffles to float gracefully.

Addie stared at herself in the mirror. She had never looked nor felt like this before. She did not feel awkward, nor too tall, nor too young. She felt delicate and feminine.

Sissy moved to stand beside her, peering at their reflections.

"I wish I had your stature. I look like a little girl playing dress up."

"You look like a lovely young woman," Addie said, and it was true. The ice-blue of Sissy's silk dress made her eyes appear almost violet. Her hair gleamed gold, and her skin was flawless, touched pink on her cheekbones by her excitement. She was small, but not childlike. Her dress was not scandalous but showed the generous swell of her breasts. She looked like an enchanting being from a fairy tale.

Addie thought that if James Fitzjohn didn't yield to Sissy's charms tonight, there was no hope for him.

The evening offered entertainment to suit different tastes. The central activity was dancing, but there were tables set up in a separate room for those who wished to play cards or other games of chance, and there were also plenty of places for quiet conversation. Food and drink were readily available, and the night was so balmy, many couples took the opportunity to stroll outside. The James River rippled with the light of the moon as if illuminated just for the festivities.

"Dancing, gambling, and staying up for all hours—not at all like home, is it?" Ad said with a grin as he came up to the girls. He had seen them descending the stairs, and he offered each an arm. "You both look very beautiful. I expect this is the last time this evening that a cousin and brother will be able to get this close to you."

Addie silently blessed him for his gallantry; she saw the added glow he'd brought to Sissy's cheeks. And he was right about the activities—Massachusetts frowned on nearly everything that was happening at Castleton tonight. Delight shimmered through her. She planned to enjoy every minute of the party, and she was thankful their father had made sure they had had dancing instruction. He was not one who saw the Devil's hand in every pleasure.

"You are looking very handsome yourself," she told her twin, and she spared a little smile for Quentin who, while relieved that he was not expected to dance, had stationed himself near the head of the stairs so he could hear the music.

The men and women of the assemblage created a garden of color in the candlelight that fell on the silks, satins, and jewels of the women, and the fine fabrics of the men's fitted knee breeches, frock coats, and elaborately embroidered waistcoats. Some of the men wore embroidered coats normally reserved for the most formal occasions such as appearances at court. And many men and women wore their hair powdered or had donned wigs to give that effect. Addie wondered if they dressed tonight in defiant statement that the highest culture could be found in the colonies as well as in England.

Ad's prediction proved correct. In short order, Sissy and Addie were swept into the dancing. The musicians were clever, varying their program from stately minuets to sprightly country dances so that both the old and the young could dance their fill.

Harry Lee partnered Addie for the "Sir Roger de Coverley," which one royal governor had renamed the "Virginia reel" for the great pleasure the colonists took in it. It was a dance of endurance as well as skill; the gentleman, without so much as touching the lady's hand, used his movements alone to guide his partner in quick steps around the room.

Harry was as adept at this as he was at riding, and Addie followed his lead until the room was a spinning whirl of light, color, and sound. When a couple tired, they dropped out, and another from the sidelines took their place, but Harry and Addie kept up until the set was over, and they were laughing with the pure energy of their performance.

"I'm fortunate you did not race today," Harry said, "else the victory might not have been mine."

Addie accepted the unconventional compliment in the same good spirit in which it had been offered. And then another young man was requesting the honor of a dance.

Like Addie, Sissy scarcely had time to catch her breath between one dance and the next, but Hart noticed that James had yet to partner her, though he had danced with other women, Cordelia among them. Cordelia was as elaborately clothed as if she were going to a ball with the King and Queen, but Hart had to admit she looked stunning in brocaded silk. She also looked entirely calculating, every smile and gesture designed to show off her charms. Hart wondered if she was aware of her partners beyond the attention they were paying to her.

He sidled over to James while Cordelia was dancing with someone else. They talked idly for a moment, and then Hart sighed heavily. "Just wait until your little sisters grow up. It's very worrying."

James blinked at him. "It is?" James's sisters were only eight and ten years old, so he hadn't considered anything about their maturity.

"It is indeed. Sissy has blossomed so suddenly, the bees, as it were, are corning in swarms."

"The bees?"

Hart wanted to shake him for being so obtuse. "Suitors. Suitors in all shapes, sizes, ages. Why, I think they range from about sixteen to sixty years old." This wasn't much of an exaggeration. Hart had noted the alarming increase in male visitors to Castleton since the family had returned from Williamsburg. They all had legitimate excuses—interest in crops or livestock or politics—but they inquired about Sissy, and about Addie also once word had gotten out that the Valencourts were visiting. Hart would leave worrying about Addie to her brothers; Sissy was concern enough.

James finally understood, and he frowned as he caught sight of Sissy surrounded by beaux vying for her attention. Far from being blind to the changes in her, he had been watching them surreptitiously for a year or more. But he had considered her too young and had been biding his time, thinking that when she reached eighteen or so, he might court her. The arrogance of his assumptions hadn't struck him until now. Somehow he had thought he would have a clear field. He had not considered that other men would see the changes as clearly as he. And tonight those changes were more visible than ever before.

Even across the room, he could see the light in her eyes, the luster of her hair, the swell of her bosom. Heat warmed his cheeks as he stared at her, and he frowned. "Surely your mother didn't know Sissy would wear such a gown tonight?"

Hart struggled to hide his triumph. "Of course she did. Haven't you been listening to me? That's the whole problem. Many are already married by her age. Sissy is a young woman now, and it's only a matter of time, and probably not much of that, before some man claims her and spirits her away from Castleton." That might be putting it too broadly, but Hart wasn't going to miss this opportunity. He was convinced his friend hadn't been as blind as he'd seemed. "I hope it is someone worthy of her. She has such a big heart, I fear she may take pity on the wrong man."

"Surely you and the rest of the family can keep her from that?"

"We will certainly try, but you know how women are, they will follow their hearts against all logic, and our parents want her to be happy above all else. They don't approve of marriages made solely for property settlements. They married for love when it was quite unfashionable to do so, and they're very happy together. They are not going to deny the same chance to Sissy, especially now with the future so treacherous." He manufactured another heavy sigh. "Ah, but you, James, have a few years before your sisters will cause you such vexation."

He risked another sideways glance and saw that James's attention was still fixed on Sissy. He didn't even seem to notice when Hart asked Cordelia to dance a gavotte with him.

Cordelia wielded her fan with languid expertise, murmuring, "It's a rather fast pace on such a warm night."

"Then may I escort you to a cooling glass of punch?" he inquired, and she went with him, praising Castleton's hospitality as they drifted through the throng. He caught a glimpse of Cordelia's mother looking very pleased with her daughter's progress, and he resolved to take care that he not replace James in Cordelia's net. He was sure Cordelia was in the market for a husband and didn't care much who he was as long as he fit the general qualifications of acceptable wealth, position, and looks. Without vanity, he knew he and James, both the oldest sons

of prominent landowners, met the requirements. And he was sure he
and his friend were interchangeable in Cordelia's mind with a host of
other young men in Virginia. The irony of it was that she would be a
good wife, dutiful and capable of managing a large household, and her
beauty would be an asset to any man. But he thought she would always
love possessions and social position more than any man. Hart did not
want a woman who would love acres and household furnishings more
than she would love him, and he didn't want James to end up with her
either. He was glad to yield his place beside her to the admirers who
approached to beg they be allowed to procure refreshment for her, and
she didn't seem to notice that Hart was dropping out of the crowd.

When James had shown no signs of noticing her, Sissy had decided
defiantly that two could play the game. She was resolved to have a
splendid time without him. And the strange thing was that she had
danced so much and had received so many extravagant compliments,
her defiance had become the truth; she had ceased to be aware of
James's presence so that when he appeared before her, she was startled
rather than pleased.

James was no less surprised. At first Sissy looked at him rather
blankly, and then if there was any emotion on her face, it was annoy-
ance, as if he had interrupted something important. He glared at
her circle of admirers, wondering which one she favored. Sissy had
always had a quick smile of welcome for him, a dancing light in her
eyes at the sight of him, even when she had been a little girl. He felt
a yawning hollow in his middle; he would have liked to believe it
was his stomach, but he thought more probably it was his heart. He
didn't want to imagine never having Sissy look at him kindly again.

His glare was fierce enough to cause her suitors to back off a pace.

"What is wrong with you?" Sissy demanded crossly. "You look
ready to spit nails! Did someone run off with Cordelia?" She could
have kicked herself for mentioning the woman, but the words were
out before she could stop them.

The hollow feeling eased a bit inside of James; she sounded jealous.
His frown eased into a smile. "I don't know where she is. I came to
request a dance with you."

As soon as they began the slow, intricate figures of a minuet, James knew it would have been better had they been dancing a fast-paced reel. She was so graceful, and when he looked down at her, he could see the ripe swell of her breasts, proof that she was all grown up. And this dance—step, glide, turn, forward and back, right and left, face to face, back to back, side to side—as formal as it was, was a courtship dance, man and woman flirting, asking, answering the questions with their bodies. He felt a jolt of pure lust that sent heat rushing through his body. Only the thought of what Hart or Reeves might do to him if they saw him slavering over their sister saved him from disgracing himself on the dance floor. After all, Hart was already worried about other men.

But as they finished, Sissy put her hand on his sleeve.

"You really do look most peculiar. Have you danced too much?" She peered up at him. She was determined not to mention Cordelia again, but she was still convinced James's strange mood had been caused by her.

He wanted to groan aloud in frustration and laugh at himself at the same time. Damn Hart for pointing out Sissy's suitors! He assured himself he would have been fine if Hart had kept his mouth shut. Then again, how he could have ignored the completeness of the change in Sissy for this long was beyond him. So familiar, but so changed. He couldn't think of any other man touching her without feeling fury pound in his head. He had never felt like this about any other female, not Cordelia or anyone else.

Sissy tugged at his sleeve, her worry unabated.

"There is nothing amiss," he lied, "but it is very warm in here." He could see the soft dew of heat on her skin. "Would you like to take a stroll outside?"

It wasn't proper, but Sissy didn't give that a second thought. She trusted James as an old friend, and dancing with him had reminded her of how much she cared for him, not for the others who had been so attentive tonight. She decided he was distracted and behaving oddly because Cordelia was allowing other men to pay attention to her. Sissy also decided she'd better take him up on his offer before Cordelia came looking for him.

The night was soft, playing its own music, muted songs from the slave quarters mixing with the harmony of night birds and crickets. Sissy and James were oblivious to other people wandering the grounds.

The moonlight turned her dress to silver, illuminated her heart-shaped face, and pooled in her eyes. James couldn't tell whether the scent of flowers came from the gardens or from Sissy.

He stared down at her, finding it difficult to draw a deep breath. Flirting with Cordelia had been amusing for both of them, but this was different. If breathing was hard, words seemed impossible.

With his head bent toward her, James's face was in shadow, but Sissy could feel his distress and was beginning to suspect this went beyond Cordelia. "What is it? Is it one of your family? They all look perfectly well, but…"

She would have chattered on in panic, but very gently, James put a finger against her lips, stilling her voice, and then just as gently he leaned down and kissed her, keeping his desire in check, testing her response, touching the corners of her mouth before he kissed her fully, and then he drew back a little.

"Oh, my word," Sissy breathed against his cheek, steadying herself by holding on to his arms.

The cloth of his coat felt real, so this must be happening. But things had changed so swiftly, she couldn't find her bearings. She had planned to capture James's affection over the coming months or even years, but tonight seeing him and Cordelia together had gone a good way toward convincing her that she had better reconsider her foolish dream. But now the dream was back, living, breathing, and feeling very big and strong beneath her hands. And he had kissed her, not like her family kissed her, not like the Breckenridge boy who had gotten a slap for his clumsy attempt the year before, not like she had ever been kissed, but…

She said the first thing that came into her head. "Could we do that again, please?"

The frozen moment between them had seemed an eternity to James, but now he laughed. "Oh, yes! We can do it again and again and again." He punctuated his words by kissing her cheeks, her nose, her eyelids, and finally her mouth, this time long and sweet. He gathered her into his arms so that her head fit against his heart, where she belonged.

As much as the idea appealed to him, they couldn't stand there kissing all night. Already someone might have seen them. He pulled himself together. He caught her hands in his and held her a little away from him.

"I'll do this properly, Sisley Anne Castleton. I'll speak to your parents, and I'll come courting as often as I can. I know this is happening very fast, and I don't want to rush you. I want to give you time to know your true feelings. But please, promise me that you won't accept any other man's offer until we've had some time together."

Sissy was about to protest that there were no others when she thought of her conversation with Hart and inwardly thanked him, though she could only imagine how he had brought James around so swiftly. Then, finally, it got through to her that James had all but asked her to marry him. She felt laughter bubbling up inside of her. If she gave in to her impulse, she would rush him. At that moment, she felt as if she knew secrets he had yet to learn. It did not matter that he had not spoken specifically of love; in essence, that was the only subject between them. They were both blessed by parents who wanted their children to be content, and in any case, the families were fairly evenly matched in wealth and influence in the colony.

"I promise I won't accept any other offers." She tried to sound solemn, but laughter danced in her voice.

James resisted the impulse to kiss her again, but he thought the sooner he began this courting business in earnest, the sooner he would be able to marry her, and do a good deal more than kiss her. And while he wasn't as political as her family, he felt that changes for the worst were in the offing. Better to be settled sooner than later.

He knew he was grinning foolishly as he led her back into the house, but he didn't care.

Hart had protected the couple, reassuring his mother when she had asked where his sister was. He hadn't lied.

"She's with James Fitzjohn, finally," he'd explained, and Catherine had said, "I see," and then she had smiled with her usual serenity.

"Your father will be as pleased as I. I'll make certain of it." It showed how much she trusted James that she went in search of her husband rather than her daughter.

Hart saw Sissy and James when they returned to the house. He didn't have to ask how things were between them; he had to pretend surprise. He lifted an eyebrow in inquiry, and James stammered, "We… she, that is. I've told Sissy that I'm going to come courting. Of course, I will speak to your parents, but I wanted to… tell you—"

Hart cut him off by giving him a hard clap on the back. "Congratulations! What a splendid idea!" He winked at Sissy who was being uncharacteristically quiet, and her mischievous little smile in return was thanks for his efforts.

But the three of them sobered when Cordelia approached. It helped that she was on the arm of a wealthy planter who had lost his wife in childbirth two years before. It helped more that Cordelia took stock of the situation quickly and handled it with grace. She betrayed no ill-will as she said, "I think Cupid has loosed his bow this night and shot true. Your smiles are brighter than the candles. Congratulations."

Sissy had never liked Cordelia as much as she did at that moment, and she felt guilty for her past bad thoughts. But she also suspected, as had her brother, that Cordelia didn't care that much for James. It was incomprehensible to her. No one was like James. But she wasn't going to point that out to Cordelia. Instead, she thanked her for her good wishes.

Sissy was touched and amused by how anxious James was to do everything properly, and he insisted he must speak to her father without delay.

"Do you want me to be with you?" she asked.

"No, I think man to man would better serve." He didn't want to admit he was nervous about the coming interview. Logic told him that his family and his prospects were acceptable, but one never knew what a father's approval might require when the father was as fond and protective of his daughter as Hartley Castleton was of Sisley Anne.

Sissy and Hart stood off to the side of the room, watching James go in search of their father.

"You don't think Papa will be harsh with him, do you?" Sissy asked, struck by the dread that after all her waiting for James to come around, everything might yet go awry.

"Mother's pleased, so Father will be, too," Hart assured her.

"Thank you for everything. I am not sure how you did it, but I give you full credit."

"I simply told him about all the suitors you have. It wasn't a lie. You would have huge swarms of them if you gave them any notice. You have too many as it is. James will be puffed up enough without knowing you'd follow him to hell if he so much as crooked his little finger. Better wait until your wedding night to tell him that."

The teasing light died out of his eyes. "Don't wait too long to wed. These are precarious times. I want you to have as many good days with James as you can."

Sissy stood on tiptoe to kiss his cheek. "I wish you had someone to love."

"So do I," Hart said, but despite the many attractions of young women he knew, he did not want to spend his life with any of them. As the eldest son, it was his duty to marry and produce an heir, but he wanted to find joy in the duty. And at present, he was more distracted by political affairs than by those of the heart.

Sissy drew Addie aside to tell her the news, her words tripping over each other. Addie shared her cousin's joy, and she was as relieved as Sissy when they saw James with Sissy's parents, all three of them looking pleased.

"I predict you'll be married before the year is out," she told Sissy.

Sissy breathed a heartfelt, "I hope so!" and went to James as if pulled by a magnet.

Addie envied her cousin. She had heard her own eyes compared to warm brandy, sherry, topaz, and precious amber. Likewise her hair was everything from honey to autumn leaves to a miracle. She had had trouble restraining her mirth over those compliments; praise of her hair seemed to present special difficulties. Her skin, mouth, hands, even her ears had received their share of flattery.

It was diverting, but none of it touched her. She didn't want to admit it, but she was as lovesick as Sissy. She wished she had been out in the moonlight with Silas. She wanted every man who complimented her to be Silas, and because none of them were, nothing they said made an impression. And because she was little distracted by them, she noticed that all through the evening, the planters, merchants, doctors, lawyers—some of them burgesses, some not, but all of them powerful men in the colony—had been drawing apart in little groups to indulge in discussions that were reflected in their serious expressions.

She felt stupid that it had taken her so many hours to understand what was going on. The bounty of Castleton had not been offered just for the sake of a good time. This was a political meeting as much as a social gathering and Addie did not doubt that word of the discussions would be carried back to people such as Colonel Washington, Richard Henry Lee, Patrick Henry, and other leaders who had obligations elsewhere, like Thomas Jefferson who had sent regrets, claiming that the fragile health of his wife prevented them from visiting Castleton.

Next month, Virginia would hold a convention to choose delegates to a congress planned for all the colonies. This assembly at Castleton had as much to do with that as it had to do with entertaining friends.

Addie thought of how happy Uncle Hartley was to be home, but she knew he would go to the convention, and she expected he would be one of the delegates chosen to represent Virginia. If so, he would be acting in defiance of the government.

Her view of this idyllic time at Castleton was radically altered within the space of minutes. This wasn't life as usual on the plantation; this was just a pause before the political fire blazed up again and threatened them all.

She maintained a pleasant façade through the rest of the party, which did not end until after breakfast the next morning, and she kept it up while she listened to Sissy telling over and over again the story of James's proposal to court her, including details of James's kisses. Sissy never failed to blush when she got to the kissing part.

But three days later, Addie told her twin, "It is time for us to go home. We can't stay here forever, and who knows what will happen once the colonies have had their meeting? The news from Boston doesn't sound so serious."

Boston might have been closed, but letters from both Marcus and Justin had reached them. Marcus was uneasy about having troops quartered in the town, but he was equally so about what the "Sons of Liberty and their ilk" might do next, so for him, the soldiers were as much reassurance as nuisance.

Justin's opinion, sent under separate cover, was wholly different. He hated having the redcoats about and believed their presence would do nothing but cause trouble. But even he had to admit that though life was more inconvenient now in the town, it was not the disaster that had been predicted.

Addie expected resistance from Ad, but he confessed, "I've been thinking the same. I wish we could leave Quentin here, though, out of the way of... of whatever is going to happen. But I don't think he'd stand for it." Ad had no intention of explaining to his sister that he was determined to join Justin and Silas in their work for the Sons of Liberty. This time in Virginia had clarified his thoughts about his rights and duties as an Englishman, had made him realize that he, unlike his father, could no longer trust the government to act for the colonies' good.

"How angry do you think Papa will be if we return before he summons us?" Addie asked.

"I don't think he'll be angry at all, at least not for long. His letter sounded lonely. With Justin so busy and not living in the house, and with us gone and Mary and the children out at the farm, I think Papa is finding the house too big and empty. For all his talk of reason and logic, Papa has a soft heart."

They dreaded telling their uncle and aunts of their decision and knew they would have a hard time traveling north without their permission and aid. But rather than resistance, they met sad and somewhat abashed agreement when they spoke to Uncle Hartley.

"The meeting in Williamsburg to choose delegates to attend the Congress in Philadelphia in September is less than a fortnight away. I think I will be among those selected." There was more resignation than pride in Hartley's voice, making it plain he did not relish leaving Castleton, or indeed Virginia, at the end of the summer when there were many crops to be harvested. "I doubt very much that your father approves of the plan for a congress in general and, in particular, he will not approve of my participation."

The twins wanted to protest that Marcus would approve this next step the colonies were taking to settle matters, but they knew it wasn't true, knew Marcus would be appalled, not only by such a meeting taking place without government sanction, but also by the radicals who would undoubtedly have their say along with the moderates.

Their uncle swallowed hard and looked away for a moment. "I have discussed this with your aunts. We would like you to stay until I leave for Philadelphia. You can travel that far north with me, and I will make sure you go on safely home. With the way events are unfolding, it may be difficult for you to return to Castleton for some time. But we want you to know you will always be welcome, whatever happens. We wish you could stay with us forever. It is not just that you are Lily's children, though God knows you bring her back to us by being here, but it is also because you've found your own places in our hearts ever since you were small children—Justin, too. Castleton is as much your heritage as it is that of your cousins."

"Thank you, Uncle," Ad said, and Addie kept her eyes very wide so that tears would not fall.

As he had predicted, Hartley attended the meeting in Williamsburg on August 1, and returned to Castleton having been chosen as one of the delegates to the Congress. It was a great tribute to him because Virginia was sending her best, among them Peyton Randolph, Richard Henry Lee, George Washington, and Patrick Henry. The Congress would begin on September 5, and Hartley wished to arrive in Philadelphia a couple of days prior to that in order to settle in. He planned to take Hart with him as his secretary.

"Do you mind not going?" Addie asked Reeves.

He was prompt to reply, "No! Hart is the politician, not I. I'm the farmer and town life holds no attraction for me. I need to learn everything I can here before I manage my own lands."

As the eldest son, Hart would inherit Castleton, but Reeves was to be well provided for with acres not far from the town of Richmond. There he would build his future. This seemed a just arrangement to him, and there was no contention between him and his brother.

For the Valencourts, the last days at Castleton spun away too quickly. Quentin drew furiously and plagued the slaves for every song and scrap of music they could recall. Ad rode as if he could already feel the narrow streets of Boston closing in around him. Addie spent time with her aunts and Sissy, but she also took advantage of long hours on horseback, needing the freedom as much as Ad did, needing to remember all the beauties as well as the complexities of Castleton because she doubted she would see it again soon.

Sissy told her that she had every hope of being married by Christmas or early in the coming year. "James isn't nearly as patient as he thinks he is," she explained, eyes gleaming with mischief as she thought of all the ways she was learning to tempt James's restraint.

True to his word, he was at Castleton often, to the point that her father had remarked that James and his horse were both beginning to look lean and worn. "Love can do that to a man," he'd observed with a reminiscent smile.

Sissy wanted Addie to witness the ceremony, to be part of it and the celebration that would follow, and they pretended that would be possible, discussing plans for the tiniest details. But as the time for the Valencourts' departure drew ever nearer, Sissy's happy pretense slipped, and tears filled her eyes.

"You're not going to be here. No matter how much you or I wish it, it's not to be. Things are just getting too difficult. It's not fair! You're more than a cousin to me; you're the sister I've never had."

Addie's own tears overflowed, and she hugged Sissy tightly. "You'll have to write to me about everything, and I'll do the same. No matter how long it is before we see each other again, we'll still be able to get word to each other." She managed a shaky laugh. "Think of Aunt Camille. Through her letters, she visits all over the colonies and England without ever leaving Virginia."

"I will have to improve my script," Sissy said, sniffing as she scrubbed at her eyes like a small child.

Chapter 5

When the day came for the Valencourts to leave Castleton, they boarded Uncle Hartley's schooner at the wharf. Catherine, Camille, Sissy, and Reeves all came to see them off. Their journey took them down the James River and up the Chesapeake to Head of Elk, whence they traveled overland to Philadelphia. The twins and Quentin had visited the pleasant Quaker city with its wide streets and neat houses before, but they didn't tarry long this time before they boarded another ship. Nor did they stop with Darius in New York. With conditions so unsettled, they wanted to get home as quickly as possible.

The first sign of change was that their ship had to dock at Marblehead because of the port of Boston being closed. It was graphic evidence of the effect of the government's punitive policy.

Uncle Hartley had sent word ahead, and he had instructed the Valencourt siblings to wait at a certain inn if no one was there to greet them. But Justin and Silas met them as they disembarked, and had been in Marblehead for two days already at Marcus's behest.

"Papa was determined you not wait for so much as an hour before being brought safely home to him," Justin told his siblings as he hugged Addie, nodded at Ad, and patted Quentin's shoulder. "That Virginia air must have something special in it. You've all grown considerably in these past months."

Addie stole a glance at Silas. He had greeted them all in his calm way, and he looked genuinely glad to see them, but Addie wanted more, and she was embarrassed at this thought. In a flash of truth, she saw herself too clearly. She'd been dreaming of him since leaving Boston, and because James Fitzjohn had tumbled so neatly into Sissy's plans, Addie had begun to imagine Silas would jump eagerly into hers. Instead, he was eyeing her with a puzzled frown, and she thought she probably looked as if she'd just bitten into a too-sour pickle. She produced a bland smile from the tatters of her pride.

"The two of you look…" She had started to say they looked well, but it wasn't so. "You look tired," she said, and concern overrode her self-consciousness. "Has it been so hard then?"

Justin glanced at Quentin and was satisfied that his attention was fixed on the nimble dance of the men unloading baggage and cargo. "It depends on one's point of view," he said. "As I wrote, Papa doesn't like the interference with business the Port Bill has caused, but he is not so unhappy about the soldiers in Boston. They give him a sense of security. I don't feel the same." He shrugged. "There's nothing for it in any case except to stay out of the redcoats' way. And that is doubly true for you, Addie. Soldiers and virtuous young women are a bad mix."

"Is Papa angry that we have come home before he sent for us?" Ad asked.

The tension eased in Justin's face as he smiled. "Actually, he's not. He's missed all of you and Mary and the children. He hasn't been out to see them as often as he wished. Tullia claims he's been driving her and the rest of the staff mad with his long face and sighs. And neither is he as angry with Uncle Hartley as you might guess. He still hopes some accommodation will be worked out with the government. Papa would not like to hear me say it, but you know he has a tender nature. He wants life to be safe and peaceful for all of us."

Unable to help herself, Addie peeked at Silas's face as Justin was speaking. Silas looked not only sad, but grim. Clearly, he had no hope that life would be either safe or peaceful for long. She looked away, wishing she could comfort him, determined that if it were not possible for him to see her as she wished, she could yet re-establish the old ease that had been between them. He did not have to know how she felt about him; for him, she would learn how to hide her heart.

The changed condition of Boston had added many complications to travel, and they spent the night with friends because it was no longer wise to try to enter the city too late in the day. They were graciously received, but even this was not easy. The stop had been selected by Marcus, and the head of the house was as much the King's man as

Marcus was, which meant that while eating a late supper, Silas and the Valencourts had to suffer through their host's bemoaning of the state to which "ruffians and smugglers" had brought Boston and the rest of New England.

Silas and Justin grew more stony-faced as the diatribe continued, but neither countered the man's opinions. Likewise the twins kept a polite silence. It was Quentin, who heretofore had seemed to have no interest in politics, who asked, "But surely, sir, the fault cannot lie entirely with the colonies?"

There was no challenge in his voice, just puzzlement, and that mollified their host.

"Well, now see here, young Quentin, well…" He hemmed and hawed before conceding, "Perhaps the government could be more discerning about conditions here. This isn't England, after all, no matter how much we might wish it. But there's no excuse for letting the rabble hold sway. That's a sure road to perdition."

Quentin did not press his point, but Addie could almost see the thoughts tumbling around in his mind. He was too young. She wanted him spared the trouble of these times. She looked across the table and saw her dread reflected in Silas's eyes.

There was no way to avoid seeing the changes when they entered Boston the next day. From the sentries who granted them passage over the narrow land of the Neck to the traffic in the winding streets, Boston was awash in redcoats. They were even camped on the Common. Some stepped to the rhythm of military drills; some marched along on official business; others strolled about off-duty. They seemed to travel in packs, as if afraid to be alone among the rebellious Bostonians.

Most fascinating to Addie was to see the soldiers with women on their arms. Some enlisted men and more officers undoubtedly had their families with them, but she was sure many of the women she saw with the soldiers were local. With an area of the town called "Mount Whoredom," there was no shortage of women of easy virtue. Before its closing, Boston had long been a thriving seaport, and the appetites of sailors and of the whores who served them were more than a match for Puritan ghosts. Addie saw one soldier casually pinch the rear of his companion, his big hand delving through the woman's skirt and petticoats, and she understood why Justin had warned her about the soldiers. However, aside from ineffectually batting at her escort's hand, the woman didn't seem too upset by his boldness. Not for the first time, Addie thought there was a great deal about this man–woman business that she had yet to learn.

Located as it was in a section of the city that was still very rural, with large houses surrounded by gardens and orchards, the Valencourt house appeared infinitely welcoming after the alien bustle in the streets. Marcus and Tullia were there to greet them, their familiar faces offering refuge.

Marcus was too delighted in his children's presence even to pretend anger at their early return. "The Castletons have taken good care of you," he said as he searched each face in turn.

He waited until later to talk to the twins about the politics of their uncle.

"I appreciate Hartley's delicacy in sending you home, but I also trust him. I cannot claim I am completely comfortable with this business of a congress, but if enough men like Hartley are delegates, surely they will follow a sensible course." He then proceeded to ask for news of each member of the Castleton family, and the twins were relieved not to be questioned about the political situation in Virginia.

Only later did it occur to Addie that this omission was deliberate. "He doesn't want to know, does he?" she asked her brother.

"No, he doesn't," Ad said. "He needs to keep believing it is merely a small band of recalcitrant New Englanders who are causing all the trouble. If it is bigger than that, if it involves people he respects, then it becomes far more complicated for him."

At that moment the twins felt as if they were parents and Marcus the child, someone to be shielded from too harsh truth. They understood how Justin and Silas had been feeling for a long time.

Addie understood something else as well. "You are going to join Justin and Silas in their work for the Sons of Liberty, aren't you?" she said to Ad.

"If they'll have me," he said.

She did not attempt to dissuade him. She knew it would be useless. Notwithstanding how she felt about this business of becoming a woman, Ad was a man now, not a boy. She did not tell him, but she had every intention of helping in whatever way she could. Steadily, the knowledge was growing within her. She was part of the New World, of the colonies, not of England. England must come to understand that while it was thousands of miles away and life here was different, the justice and rights due its citizens should be the same as those granted to the people who lived much closer to Westminster.

As frustrating as it was, Addie knew the best thing she could do for the moment to help her brothers and Silas was to give them no cause to worry about her.

Marcus's plan had long been for Ad to learn all aspects of the Valencourt enterprises, and he had learned a great deal since he had finished college, though he had not worked at the shops on a regular basis. Marcus had understood how disruptive his new marriage could be to Lily's children, and he also understood how strong the bond between the twins was. The family had needed Ad more at home than in the bookstore or printing office. But now it was time for Ad to go to work in earnest. The plan suited Ad and his father equally but for different reasons. Marcus was holding to his old vision of having Justin take over in Boston when the time was right while Ad would open another branch of Valencourt's in Philadelphia. He had thought so far ahead as to imagine Quentin presiding over yet another in Annapolis or Williamsburg, or perhaps even Charlestown in South Carolina. And if Mary's son Peter was interested, there would be a place for him, too. Marcus refused to consider that the current unsettled political climate would have any lasting effects on business or anything else. After all, he had made a great deal of money during the French and Indian War when, like many other merchants, he had obtained lucrative contracts to supply various goods to the army. That time of unrest had been of benefit, so perhaps something good would come of this time also.

Ad's goals were not so farsighted. He simply wanted to be close to his older brother and Silas and involved in their clandestine work. Like his sister, Ad had gradually clarified his ideas about what was and was not owed to the colonies by the mother country. The sight of redcoats swanning so boldly in possession of Boston had been an immediate shock. The presence of British soldiers was not new. They had been garrisoned in the town until removed to Castle William after the Boston Massacre four years ago. But Ad had been younger then, unconcerned about political ferment, and this current occupation seemed far more menacing, far more of a trespass. Now when Ad looked at the soldiers, he saw a foreign presence, a possible enemy. He had begun to think of himself as an American, not an Englishman.

While it was possible to pass by the soldiers in the street without making direct contact, quite the opposite was true at work. Valencourt's Book and Stationery Store had long been a fashionable place for the town gentry to meet as they perused current titles and the classics and the host of other goods, and the officers of the latest governor, General Thomas Gage, quickly chose it as a favored meeting place, often coming with their wives or other female companions. They also frequented the printing office next door, ordering invitations for special occasions such as a supper at this or that officers' mess or a musical evening or such, creating their own social life in a city not known for its carousing.

Ad watched Justin and Silas and learned from them. They were unfailingly polite to their customers, and they listened to everything they said.

Ad's determination to join Justin in the Sons of Liberty led inevitably to a clash between the brothers.

"It's too damned dangerous! And you're too young!" Justin stormed. "You're a poor liar and might easily betray us to Papa or, worse, to the redcoats."

"As I betrayed you last year when you and Silas helped to dump the tea?" Ad asked calmly.

Justin stared at him, and Ad nodded. "Addie and I saw you. We were at Old South when the 'Mohawks' ran past." He did not explain that Silas had seen them. "And while I was in Virginia, I drilled with Hart and Reeves. I know you would like to protect me, but you can't, not any more than I can protect you. I'm seventeen, no longer a child.

I have the same right as you to resist tyranny that will shape my future unless it is stopped now."

Justin bowed his head, knowing he had no choice about accepting Ad's decision; his brothers and his sister, they were free thinkers, each one in his or her way.

Before long, Ad accompanied Justin and Silas to a meeting of the leaders of the Sons of Liberty at the Green Dragon Tavern. Quite a few of the men were known to Ad, including Dr. Church, an apothecary and physician, and Mr. Revere, a silversmith, and he was treated with special deference for having returned recently from Virginia. It was desperately important to these men that leaders in other colonies stand by Boston in her time of need. Their great hope lay in the Congress. Except for Georgia, whose royal governor had persuaded representatives not to go to Philadelphia, all of the colonies had sent delegates.

Aware of all eyes upon him, Ad made an effort to speak smoothly. "There are differences in opinion in Virginia, as there are here. But many powerful Virginians are just as determined as you are that their rights as Englishmen be preserved. And most of them see the government's treatment of Boston as a threat to Virginia. I know the men in the Virginia delegation; our uncle is one of them, and now that Peyton Randolph has been chosen as president of the Congress, that can only deepen the delegation's involvement." He forwent pointing out what everyone knew, that Samuel and John Adams, the most influential of Massachusetts's delegates, had undoubtedly helped engineer the selection of Randolph for just that reason. But when he thought of those rather forbidding and fanatical New Englanders in comparison with the Virginians, he could not repress his misgivings.

"I am sure you are aware of this, but I feel obliged to mention it," he said, and now there was a quaver of uncertainty in his voice. "While there are many ideals in common, Virginians and New Englanders seem very different to me. Their lives are different. Virginians are far more dependent on trade with England than we are. They have much at stake."

No one argued with him, and Mr. Revere said, "Well put. If the Virginians do side with us, we will know how true their dedication is."

Justin noted the glitter in his brother's eyes even after the meeting had adjourned, and said, "I know this must be exciting for you. But all we're doing is waiting and watching. The militia is gathering ordnance at various points. Despite their best efforts, these stores aren't much of a secret, and many of us think General Gage won't let such preparations go on forever. A lot depends on the Congress and on Parliament, on whether they can establish some common ground. So in the meantime, your biggest job will be to skulk in alleys and avoid redcoats."

Ad gave him an impudent grin. "Then I'll aim at becoming a superior skulker."

Silas had kept silent, but now he said, "You'll make sure Addie doesn't get involved, won't you?"

His voice was so anxious, Ad looked at him in puzzlement. "I'm not going to let her sneak around with me at night, and I don't think she'll try; she grew up a lot in Virginia. But as for keeping her from knowing what's going on, that's impossible. Why don't you tell her you're concerned? She thinks highly of you."

To Ad's further amazement, Silas flushed dark red and stalked off without another word.

"What in the world is the matter with him?"

"What would you guess?" Justin asked in turn and watched with amusement as an explanation occurred to his brother.

"Silas is in love with Addie! Well, damn, that's perfect!"

"I think so, too, but it's Silas's secret. This is one case where you cannot confide in Addie. Silas is determined to sacrifice himself on the altar of honor; he doesn't believe he's worthy of our sister."

"But that's ridiculous! He's—"

"Exactly." Justin didn't let him finish. "He is an exceptional man, and no one could be a better match for Addie. But I mentioned it to him once, and we nearly came to blows. So we're going to have to keep our mouths shut and hope things work out as they should. That's assuming, of course, that Addie has similar feelings for Silas. You wouldn't happen to know about that, would you?"

"As close as we are, we've never talked about that sort of thing. But I can tell you our sister attracted more than her share of admirers in

Virginia. She didn't seem to pay them much notice, though, so maybe that means she's interested in Silas." Ad rubbed a hand over his face. "Then again, maybe it means she's not ready to choose anyone yet. I don't know enough about this subject!"

"Comes to that, neither do I," Justin confessed. "Sarah's not only older than Addie. She's... she's tamer somehow. She wants a home and a settled life. Our Addie is different, wilder inside, I think."

They exchanged identical looks of males confounded by trying to fathom the females in their lives.

But before they parted, Justin had a final warning for his brother. "Take care. Papa has dined with General Gage, and I hear some of Gage's officers are beginning to feel quite at home visiting the house. Doing business with them is one thing, entertaining them socially is another. If any had doubts about Papa's loyalties before, they have none now. Watch yourself around those visitors. Not all redcoats are as stupid and bumbling as the broadsides would make them."

Ad envied Justin and Silas the freedom of living over the shops but he felt too protective of his twin and Quentin to move out of the house. He shared Justin's unease regarding the uniformed visitors.

Support for their feelings came from an unexpected quarter. Mary and the children returned from the farm because Mary refused to be separated from Marcus any longer.

In order to come back into the city, she had agreed to have little Clement inoculated against smallpox, and Marcus had arranged for a skilled physician to perform the operation. Mary had then had to wait until the minor form of the disease had run its course to ensure any unprotected people would not be exposed to it. Despite the controversy surrounding the procedure and the sporadic legal measures passed against it, Marcus had long been an advocate and all his family were inoculated. In both England and the colonies, Marcus had seen what the disease could do if unchecked, and he was doubly determined to protect his family these days because smallpox accompanied armies as if it were a standard part of their equipment. Silas had had the disease and so was immune, Tullia had also been inoculated, and Marcus had done his best to encourage the same in all his staff.

Passing his father's library one day after his stepmother's return, Ad was so shocked to hear Mary's normally soft voice raised in agitation that for a moment, he couldn't believe it was hers.

"I risked our baby's life to protect him from the pox! I allowed him to be inoculated because I trusted your good judgment. But you are showing none now! Have you taken leave of your senses? This house is becoming known as a place where redcoats are always welcome. You even dare to serve tea to them! You are choosing sides as clearly as if you had posted a sign."

Marcus's voice was mild in contrast to hers. "Most of the officers have been recommended to us by my daughter Callista and her husband. Having known them or their families in England, they wanted them to receive some kindness so far from their homes. As for choosing sides, what sides do you speak of? The soldiers are the legitimate members of His Majesty's forces. I have made no choice. I am, as I have always been, an Englishman loyal to the Crown and Parliament."

"Oh, husband! You are being deliberately blind! You should have spent more time out in the country with us. Then you would have been forced to see. The militia is drilling everywhere. This resistance to the government is not the work of a few! It has become the cause of the many who call themselves Patriots. And they are angry. You know what has happened to some of the government's supporters in the past when tempers ran high. Men have been tarred and feathered, ridden through the streets on a rail, and heaven knows what else. It is worse now. By your actions, you make yourself, indeed all of us, targets for their wrath. Why could you not show a neutral face?"

"There is no need. The King's troops are here to protect his loyal subjects as much as to restrain those who are disloyal."

The fury died out of Mary's voice, but the weary resignation that replaced it was more chilling to Ad as he remained frozen in place, listening. "The King's troops are here but scarce any place else. They might as well be prisoners of this town; mayhap they are. And we with them."

It was the sound of her quiet sobbing and his father's crooning attempts to comfort her that finally broke the spell for Ad and sent him scurrying away. He was ashamed he had eavesdropped so long, and he told no one, not even Addie, but what he had heard haunted him. He liked Mary well enough but had not thought of her as a person in her own right; she had simply been his father's wife. Now he understood that she was as full of conflict as he was. She came from stock that had been in Massachusetts for more than a hundred years. For the first time, it occurred to him that his stepmother's loyalties might not coincide with her husband's. It made him feel sorry for his father.

Addie didn't have to eavesdrop to gather that Mary was unhappy with the red-coated visitors. She spent more time than ever with her children, and when she could not avoid guests save by being overtly rude, she was so reserved as to become nigh invisible in her home. But in small, purposeful rebellion, she would not drink tea—coffee or chocolate, but not tea.

One day Addie even heard her say, when an officer thought she had forgotten to pour for herself, "No, thank you. I find tea no longer agrees with my constitution. It has not for some time."

The officer gave her a hard look, which Mary met with a bland smile, as if political protest was the furthest thing from her mind.

Addie handled the situation less gracefully. On a similar occasion, she gave an elaborate shudder, made a face, and announced, "I never could stand the stuff! It reminds me of being quite deathly ill when I was a child and tea thick with honey was offered as a cure." There wasn't a word of truth in that—she would have liked to have a whole pot to herself—but no gentleman would question such a forceful statement.

Addie felt closer to Mary than she ever had, but she did not confide in her or ask her where her loyalties lay. Instead, she tried to help by acting as substitute hostess, though always deferring to Mary lest the older woman think she was trying to supplant her.

Mary soon made it plain she was grateful to Addie for stepping in, but she offered a caution. "Be careful how you go with these young officers, my dear. They are far enough from home that they might have left their manners behind. And you are beautiful enough to tempt any man, manners or no."

Addie was so startled by this pronouncement, Mary smiled ruefully. "You've spent too much time in the company of your brothers. They're not apt to turn your head with compliments. But..." She gave a little shake of her head. "Oh, never mind. You are a sensible young woman with no need of advice from me."

Addie knew Mary was withdrawing into her habitual role of not interfering with her stepchildren. But for the first time, it seemed a difficult role for her, and that was surely a measure of how worried she was about the soldiers visiting.

"I appreciate your concern," Addie assured her and left it at that.

Reluctantly, Addie found that she admired some of the officers. Many were from good families, but being younger sons, unless they emigrated, as Marcus had done, they had little choice beyond the clergy or the army. And in both of those establishments advancement depended far more on friends in powerful positions than on personal merit. Plus, in the army, advancement also carried a high monetary cost determined by what rank in which regiment one wanted to obtain. If one had enough influence and money, it was possible to glean the honors of appointment without ever spending a day with one's regiment.

"Of course, it is much easier to move up if men are dying in battle, leaving their positions to be filled by others."

Captain Paul Byrne had become a regular visitor, and Addie had grown accustomed to the dark humor that sometimes colored his words.

"What? Are you not going to berate me for broaching such an inelegant subject?" he goaded her.

"No. I expect what you say is true. I can hardly chide you for that. But it must be terrible to be in the army if you hate it so much."

The pose of cynicism fell away suddenly, and his pain was revealed. "Ah, but there's the rub. I don't hate it; I love it. I love the long tradition of brave men fighting for England. I love the common soldiers who put up with so much for so little recompense. Now they must pay from their small wages for food, uniforms, equipment, for everything which ought to be granted them for bearing arms for the King. What

I do hate is the system of patronage and plunder that is crippling the army and the navy both. I—" He broke off and gazed at Addie for a long moment before he said, "I vow, there is something about you that makes it too easy for me to speak words better left unsaid."

"Perhaps they are better said than kept inside to eat away at you." Addie spoke softly and kept her expression sympathetic, but inside she felt a rush of triumph. This was something she could do, this listening and drawing out of the redcoats. And the more they trusted her, the more careless they would become in what they said.

The only drawback to this was that in the case of Captain Byrne, particularly, she genuinely liked him. He was well educated, observant, witty. He was twenty-five with flaxen hair, pale-blue eyes, and a rather long face. Above medium height, he moved with graceful precision. She had heard another officer praising his fencing skill, and she expected he would be equally proficient at dancing. He was a grenadier and, as in the colonial militia, they were chosen for their better than average size and athletic prowess.

She admitted to herself that in normal circumstances, she might be very attracted to him. But nothing was normal now, and she owed her loyalty to her brothers and to Silas and beyond them, to their shared belief that oppression of the colonies must cease.

The factor she didn't want to examine too closely was how pleasing it was to have someone like Captain Byrne paying such attention to her when Silas seemed to be making every effort to avoid her. Because of this, she gave few personal details about the captain to Ad when she related what he and the other soldiers had said.

Ad was especially interested in talk of discontent. "If enough British officers feel that way, it must surely diminish their capabilities in the colonies."

"It isn't just discontent with the army," Addie pointed out, "it is also with the idea of punishing the colonies. I believe it makes many of the officers uneasy. Some have direct ties to relatives here, and others just don't like the idea of threatening fellow Englishmen. Some come from Whig families." She thought of Captain Byrne but did not say his name. His father was a Whig in Parliament and continued to be outspoken in his rebuke of government policy toward the colonies. The captain had been open about it, going so far as to admit that his father had asked that he refuse being posted to Boston. But the captain, as an honorable soldier, could not do that.

Rather than being optimistic about this, Ad shrugged. "I expect Whigs in the army are as much a minority as they are in Parliament."

Addie couldn't dispute that, and she remembered something else she had wanted to tell her brother. "We've had one visitor I find rather odd. He's in civilian dress, but he carries himself like a soldier—I'm becoming adept at spotting that. He speaks perfect English, but there is a small trace of an accent. He's a Scotsman, a Highlander by the name of John Traverne. Callista recommended him to Darius, whom he visited recently in New York, and Darius bid him visit us. He has said little about his business, only that the Highlands are losing too many people to the colonies. There has been famine and other hardships in the past few years, but mostly it is a matter of the clan system being destroyed after the Highlanders lost at Culloden nearly thirty years ago, or so he says. His family would like the traffic to go the other way, back to the Highlands."

"That sounds reasonable," Ad said, but there was doubt in his voice.

"Does it? A Highlander traveling colony to colony at this time, apparently at ease with English authorities. A man who wears ordinary clothes but bears himself like a soldier? The officers who visit seem to defer to him instinctively, though he can't be much older than twenty-three or four. He's—" She was going to say "dangerous" but thought better of it because she didn't know how to explain it to Ad.

John Traverne was a big man with thick black hair worn unpowdered and eyes so dark a blue they sometimes looked black, too. His skin was weathered, his bones so strong, he made Captain Byrne appear rather delicate in comparison. And though Traverne displayed perfect manners, Addie could too easily imagine him wrapped in tartan and wielding a claymore. But her more immediate problem was that she could feel him watching and listening as intensely as she. It was disconcerting.

"He's very observant," Addie continued, "as if he's very interested in the situation here." She sighed in frustration. "That doesn't explain anything."

"Perhaps it does," Ad said thoughtfully. "There are thousands of men from Scotland and Ireland in the colonies. And a good number of them were soldiers before they settled here after the last war ended. Many of them live on the frontiers in the most hazardous places. If it comes to armed conflict, they, particularly the Highlanders, would be strong fighters on whichever side they chose."

"So perhaps he is here to judge where their loyalties lie," Addie continued his thought. "And if that is so, Highlander or not, he has the sanction of the government."

"And maybe we are both making up stories to scare ourselves," Ad offered, but he planned to talk to Justin immediately.

"Maybe." Addie didn't sound any more convinced than Ad felt. But even if this Traverne was an agent for the government, there was nothing that could be done about it.

"I think you're in more jeopardy during the social calls at the house than we are sneaking about at night."

Ad's longing for more excitement was so obvious, Addie snapped at him, "You ought to pray it never comes to more than that! Do you know that Tullia waits up most of the nights when you are gone?"

Tullia hadn't said a word about Ad's nocturnal prowling, but the twins had no doubt she had a good idea of what he was doing; she always did.

"So do you," Ad said gently, "and I wish neither of you would. It doesn't help me to know you're losing sleep." He stared off into space. "I wonder how long it will take for the government to respond to the actions of the Congress."

The Congress had adjourned on October 26 and resolved to meet again the following May if their grievances were not redressed by the government. It had issued important state papers, including those that denounced the Coercive Acts and advised people to arm themselves and form their own militia. They had framed a Declaration of Rights listing the personal rights—life, liberty, property, assembly, and trial by jury—to which colonists, as Englishmen, were entitled. This declaration also called for a repeal of many laws passed by parliament in the past eleven years. It had also passed the "Continental

Association," which was aimed at pressuring Britain economically by calling for nonimportation and nonconsumption of British goods and the nonexportation of American products, except rice, to Britain or the West Indies. And in order to garner support for their efforts, the Congress had issued petitions to the King and to the people of England and America.

The Congress had been bold in its actions, so much so that moderates were feeling aggrieved and apprehensive, sure that things had gone too far. Hart had written to the twins in this vein before the Congress adjourned. While he was pleased by the actions taken, he noted that his father was not.

> Papa feels the radicals from New England had too much to do with this business, but it seems to me that less forceful efforts have already been tried and have failed.

The problem was complicated by the time it took for petitions and declarations to cross the sea and for Parliament to respond. Meanwhile, tensions grew as the British Army paraded in Boston and the provincial militia drilled out in the countryside.

"I don't know quite what I expected, but it wasn't this endless waiting," Ad confessed. "It wears on the nerves."

"It's wearing on the redcoats, too, from what I hear them say." Addie cast about for a subtle way to question Ad about Silas, but the best she could do was to ask bluntly, "Justin and Silas, they are all right? We scarcely see them here any more." Her dilemma was compounded by the fact that though she would see Justin if she went to the bookstore, Silas was usually in the printing office, and it was difficult to think of an excuse to seek him out there. In the past, she would have dropped in to see him without a second thought, but now she shied away from being so forward.

"It is enough for them to serve the redcoats as customers," Ad said. "They don't want to break bread with them. And Justin spends his free time with Sarah Goodwin these days. I think he intends to marry her before too long." When his sister paid no attention to this announcement, Ad's suspicion that her real interest was in Silas was confirmed, but he did not quiz her about it.

Ad reported what Addie had told him about the redcoats and the Scotsman to Justin and Silas, and Silas asked, "What was that name again?"

"Traverne."

"Traverne's Highlanders fought with us against the French and Indians in the war. They were disbanded at the end of it, and some settled in this country, in Massachusetts, New York, and further south, too. How old is this man?"

"Addie guesses about twenty-three or four," Ad said.

Neither he nor Justin doubted Silas's information. Silas had long had an interest in the war, because his father had died in it, and had acquired a detailed knowledge of the campaigns and regiments.

"If he's from the same family, he must be a young relation of the brigadier general who commanded those Scots," Silas said slowly as he thought about it. "I hope he is here for an innocent purpose, but nothing seems innocent to me these days. Highlanders have a well-earned reputation for being among the most ferocious fighters anywhere. I would not like to know that there is a plan afoot to bring them against us."

In the silence that followed his words, the three young men realized they were thinking as if armed conflict were a certainty.

"I worry about Addie. It seems harmless, just listening, but I don't know. Those officers aren't blind, and I think some of them are beginning to pay serious attention to her. It isn't so extraordinary. General Gage has spent nearly twenty years in the colonies, has extensive land holdings in New York, and is married to an American-born woman with whom he has a clutch of children. Of course, I am assuming the officers are honorable..." Ad let his voice trail off with just the right amount of doubt. It had come to him while he was speaking about his real concern that it wouldn't do any harm for Silas to know that Addie was no child to other men.

Justin's eyes locked with his brother's for an instant of amused understanding before he said, "I don't like it any more than you do, but I think we have to trust Papa and Tullia to keep watch. And Addie is a sensible girl. I can't imagine her being charmed into doing anything she does not want to do."

Silas's snort of derision was so audible, the brothers couldn't ignore it.

"Don't you trust Addie?" Justin asked.

"I trust *her*, but I don't trust redcoats!" Silas barked. "Maybe we ought to visit the house more often." He stated this as if he and Justin hadn't discussed all the reasons for avoiding the house unless absolutely necessary.

"Maybe we should," Justin returned. "We might learn more about Addie's mysterious Scotsman."

Ad concentrated on showing no reaction.

The Highlander was not there when the young men joined the family for Sunday dinner, having bid the family farewell the day before, but Captain Byrne was in attendance, invited by Marcus. Ad and Justin needed no further proof of Silas's feelings for their sister than his behavior that afternoon. Usually he handled himself well whatever the circumstance, but this day he had scarcely a word to say, and he watched Addie like a hawk.

Addie was delighted to see him, but her joy turned swiftly to dismay. She had never seen Silas behave so boorishly, and the last thing she wanted was for Captain Byrne to suspect him of harboring sentiments against the government. She assumed having to share a family meal with a British officer was what was making him behave so strangely.

Finally she had had enough. "May I speak with you for a moment, Silas?" she asked sweetly after the meal was finished. But once they were alone, her sweetness turned to fire. "What possesses you? Whether you like it or not, Captain Byrne is a guest in this house! You have no right to be so rude. And it is dangerous."

"Whether *you* like it or not is more to the point," he flared back. "Captain Byrne seems much at home here, and I am sure you are most of the reason for that!"

Addie had never known Silas to be angry with her—concerned about her safety because of various escapades with Ad, but never angry. There was no mistaking his fury. His eyes glittered, his mouth was drawn in a thin line, and the cords in his neck were rigid under his skin. She saw a pulse beating on one side of his forehead. Despite ingrained trust, for an instant she feared him as he towered over her. Then her rage bubbled higher at the thought of his disparaging tone and what he was implying, as if she were no better than the doxies who plied their wares with the soldiers.

"Callista recommended Captain Byrne to us. He is a pleasant man who has acted with perfect civility toward me and everyone else in this house. I feel guilty that I am so willing to spy on him and to pass whatever I hear to you and my brothers. But I am willing. I have not lost sight of my beliefs nor of my purpose," Addie spit the words out one by one.

Silas hardly heard them. He had seen that flash of fear, and it had seared across his heart. He was raving like a jealous fool. All his noble intentions of standing apart from Addie had been based on his certainty that she would find some man of higher education and standing than he, but he had not bargained on a British officer. As long as the troops were quartered in Boston to punish the city and the colony, Silas would regard them as enemies. And the last thing he would give up to them was Addie.

He looked down at her face, at her golden eyes sparking with anger, at her full mouth that trembled slightly, at the soft skin, and he saw everything physical and beyond that made her unique.

He breathed her name, not "Addie," but "Ariadne," and then very, very gently, he kissed her. He wanted to fold her into his arms and keep her there, but he made himself draw away. He felt as much despair as love. He had so little to offer her, and all of it had come from her father.

Addie heard him groan, "Oh, God!" and she didn't know whether it was curse or prayer. And then he was gone, leaving her standing there in shock. She pressed her fingers against her mouth, still feeling his kiss. Such a soft touch to create such a strong reaction. Her blood was singing through her veins. Now she understood how Sissy had felt the night of the party at Castleton. But this was different and much more confusing. Silas was jealous; he was jealous because he had strong feelings for her. But he didn't welcome those feelings. And he'd quit the house so abruptly, she was left to conjure reasons for his disappearance.

She tried to recapture her anger, but it was gone. She suspected she looked as dazed as she felt when she rejoined the others. "Silas had to… uh, that is, he remembered something he had to do."

Silas had been so surly, no one expressed regret about his departure, but Addie felt compelled to explain further to Captain Byrne as he took his leave. "Silas behaved badly today, and that is not at all like him."

Far from being annoyed, the captain was amused. "You needn't offer excuses. I think I must feel flattered that your friend views me as a rival for your attention." He studied her face, and she felt as if he could see Silas's kiss. "But he doesn't have to worry, does he?"

It was an intimate, improper question, but she answered honestly. "No, he does not have to worry."

"I never thought to play such a part, but perhaps your Silas needs a little prodding from competition." His smile was wry. "I hope he knows how fortunate he is. Good day, Mistress Valencourt."

"Good day, Captain." Considering how jumbled her thoughts were, she was proud of the calm tone of her voice. But when Ad and Justin approached her with expectant looks, she shook her head. "I am not going to say one word about Silas's behavior. Speak to him if you wish to know what perturbs him."

"This matchmaking is frustrating business," Justin remarked to Ad as their sister stalked off. "After that performance, Papa must know that Silas cares for Addie. The question is whether or not Silas will act on his feelings. He's stubborn. He'd deprive himself and Addie of contentment if he thought it was the right thing to do."

"I don't think we can do any more for them," Ad said, regretting that it was no longer as easy to make his sister happy as it had been when they were children.

Addie didn't tell anyone about the kiss, not even Sissy when she wrote to her to wish her joy in her wedding planned for Christmas.

But she thought of it constantly, closing her eyes and trying to recreate the exact sensation she'd had.

Tullia regarded her suspiciously and shook her head, mumbling, as if it were an incantation, "Too many secrets in this house." But from the sly gleam in Tullia's eyes, Addie suspected she approved of this secret.

Addie didn't seek out Silas. She waited patiently. Serenity settled in her heart. He was jealous. He had kissed her. He was a man of deep emotions seldom revealed. She had to trust him to come to the right decision. Indeed, he visited more often, though always with Justin or Ad, and he made sure he was not alone with her. He was more polite to other company, even to Captain Byrne, than he had been on that fateful Sunday, but his eyes betrayed him, watching Addie constantly.

As the year drew to a close, plans were made for Justin and Sarah to marry right before Christmas. Under the circumstances of an occupied city, a grand affair seemed tasteless, even to Marcus. Political troubles or no, Congregationalists disliked frivolity at Christmas, seeing in it a mishmash of pagan practices, but the Anglicans were not so staid, and if they weren't so expansive as those in Virginia, at least they could indulge in good food and drink without guilt.

Addie could imagine the party Sissy and James were going to have for their wedding at Castleton, and she wished she could have gone south to witness it. But it was sufficient compensation to see her brother wed.

Sarah Goodwin obviously adored Justin, and Addie didn't doubt she would be a good wife to him, but it troubled her that Sarah's parents were of like mind with Marcus.

"They don't know you are a member of the Sons of Liberty, do they?" she asked Justin.

"Of course they don't!"

"And Sarah?"

He hesitated over this before he explained, "Sarah isn't like you. She doesn't think independently. When we are married, her loyalty will be to me, not to her parents. She knows I do not approve of the government's actions, but that is not of much concern to her."

It will be when you're out prowling at night and if you take up arms against the government, Addie thought, but she refrained from saying it aloud. It was unimaginable to her that a man and woman could be happy together if they did not share ideas or at least discuss them. But she knew that many couples, perhaps most, existed just that way, with the women caring for domestic matters and the men dealing with the outside world. She reminded herself that Sarah would take good care of Justin. This was a marriage of choice, not of commerce.

Sarah's father was a prosperous merchant dealing in dry goods and hardware, selling a range of items from the smallest household utensil to furniture, paintings, and such. Despite the closing of Boston, Mr. Goodwin, like Marcus, was not having business problems yet, proof he had laid in an ample supply of merchandise before the Port Bill took effect.

As would be expected, the young couple was receiving generous gifts from both families. Marcus purchased a substantial brick house for them in the fashionable North End, where Sarah's family lived, and Mr. Goodwin was furnishing the interior. And both families contributed to a lavish set of silver, which included everything from flatware to serving pieces to teapot and punch bowl. Though the design was English, the maker was Mr. Revere, a fact that provided Justin with wry inner amusement when he thought of how his father and father-in-law would react if they knew they had provided profit to a radical Whig. The silver was not only ornamental and useful for its shaped purpose, it was also precious for its metal. There was always a shortage of hard money in the colonies; a silver service was as good as having a hoard of coins in one's house.

Two days before Christmas, Addie watched Justin and Sarah exchange their vows in Christ Church, where the Goodwins worshiped. She thought they looked like any other young couple starting a new life together, as if no special dangers lurked in their future. They both looked so beautiful, tears swam in her eyes.

Silas was among the small group of witnesses. He felt joy for the couple—and envy. When Justin intoned, "With this ring I thee wed, with my body I thee worship, and with all my worldly goods I thee endow," Silas winced inside. He wanted to make the same vow to Addie, but his "worldly goods" were so limited as to be shameful in comparison to the wealth in Addie's family.

He had managed to make sure Ad was between himself and Addie as they watched the ceremony, but he was close enough to see the sheen of tears in her eyes. He knew they were not for herself, but this marriage would bring a major change to Addie's life. Now that Justin would be living with Sarah in the newly purchased house, Silas would move to the quarters over the printing office, since he spent most of his time in that shop these days, and Ad would move into the rooms above the bookstore. Addie would still have family around her, but Silas knew that wouldn't be the same at all. Quentin was three years younger and lived in his own world, and while Addie was fond of her stepmother and the younger children, they were essentially a separate family. Silas didn't want to think about it, but it distressed him that Addie would be lonely without her twin, though it was natural that Ad have more independence. And he couldn't help but think that he himself would see even less of her now because, although he would be welcome, he couldn't imagine accompanying the bridal pair to Sunday dinner like a bachelor uncle, and he wasn't as close to Ad as to Justin so that going with him would seem awkward, too. And then he thought that perhaps it was his loneliness he was feeling, not Addie's.

He did go to Christmas dinner at the Valencourt house. He ate of the rich food and toasted the King and the Queen with fine wine. He saw how besotted Justin and Sarah were with each other. And he saw how beautiful Addie looked dressed in deep-green velvet, warm against the damp chill of December. The green made her eyes seem more gold than ever. She was animated, happy to have her family together, and far from ignoring him, Silas found she made sure he was included in the conversation. It was as if the kiss had never happened. He knew her attitude was the most sensible course. And it infuriated him. It made his jealousy boil up again. Maybe she had been kissed so often, his effort hadn't meant anything. He saw the injustice of that; Addie was no casual flirt. That made him feel worse. Maybe his kiss had meant nothing to her because it hadn't made her feel anything special. Would that he had been so fortunate.

When he was preparing to leave, she came to him. Putting her hand on his coat, she said, "Silas, forgive me for saying so, but you do not look well. If you are sickening, please let Tullia brew one of her potions for you. They may taste dreadful, but they work."

It was all he could do not to jerk his arm away. He could feel her hand burning through the cloth to his skin. "Thank you for your concern, but I am well." He was so coldly formal, she stepped back.

"I will have to take your word for it. But you are too independent sometimes, you know. Please don't be stubborn about this if you need aid."

It would have been easier for him if she had gotten angry at him for his rudeness, but instead, she continued to regard him with worry. He wondered what she would do if he told the truth, if he told her he couldn't eat nor sleep for thinking of her, more specifically for thinking of making love with her. He thought he might be going mad. He thought the only sane thing to do was to stay away from her until the madness passed. He wondered how many years that would take.

He lasted one week. On New Year's Day, the Valencourt house was open to visitors, including soldiers of the King. But that wasn't enough to stop Silas. He even managed to greet Captain Byrne civilly, though the man's knowing look set his teeth on edge. As soon as there was an interval between visitors, he asked Addie if he might see her alone.

He looked more haggard than he had the week before, but she forwent mentioning it. It was difficult, but Addie meant to stay the course of leaving Silas to make his decision about the two of them, and she would abide by whatever he chose.

She eyed him warily. Thinking only of privacy, she had led him to the same room where he had kissed her, and now she wished she had chosen some other place. But her embarrassment was swept away by a jolt of fear when she saw how grave he looked.

"What is it? Not Justin or Sarah? You wouldn't have waited to tell us, would you? They're due to come here later in the day. They—"

"Nothing is amiss with them. I'm sorry to frighten you. I... My God, this is even harder than I thought it would be!" He studied her face. He saw the soft light in her eyes, and suddenly the words were easy. "I don't want you to marry Captain Byrne. I love you, Ariadne Valencourt. I didn't mean to, but I do. I have little to offer you, and all of it has come from your father. There is shame in that. And we could not marry until we know what will happen with the government. If things go badly, I will of a certainty lose my position at Valencourt's. I'm a good pressman, compositor, and bookbinder, but those skills may not be enough to... and I may have to go for a soldier anyway. I am a member of the militia, and that means..."

Addie stilled his voice by cradling his face in her hands.

"Do I have anything to say about this?" she asked. "You seem to be declaring your love and talking yourself out of it at the same time. Don't you want to know how I feel?" Laughter mixed with her tears, and she thought of how it had taken a gathering of Virginia notables to bring James Fitzjohn to his senses regarding Sissy, while it needed only one redcoat to bring Silas to the mark.

He nodded, and she kissed him, as he had kissed her.

"I love you, Silas Bradwell, no other man. You must be blind, for Captain Byrne saw the truth just by the way I look at you. We love each other, that is all that matters."

Silas put his arms around her and held her close to his heart. He breathed in the soft flowery scent of her skin and hair. He gloried in how well she fit against him, tall enough so that her head rested right beneath his chin. He thought of having her beside him for a lifetime, and his throat closed, his eyes filled with tears for the brief, perfect vision.

It was impossible to hold to it; truth intruded too readily. All summer and fall, General Gage had been welcoming reinforcements. Now there were four thousand British soldiers in Boston and at Castle William. Broadsides attacking Gage and his troops were being published in ever greater numbers, and Silas and Justin were responsible for many of them in the city. So-called "minutemen" were drilling out in the countryside and were ready to leave their homes, shops, and farms at a moment's notice to defend their rights as Englishmen.

Addie would have married him immediately, but she would not force him to act against his conscience. It was enough that love was acknowledged between them; surely it would not be long before Silas saw that marriage was the next logical step, in spite of the complications of politics.

She felt the sudden tension in him, and she murmured, "All will be well, it will. We'll find a way to make it so."

She did not protest when he held her so tightly her gown was crushed and she could hardly breathe. As tall and strong as Silas was, she wanted to wrap herself around him and shield him from all harm.

Chapter 6

Spring 1775

Far from settling down, relations between the soldiers and citizens grew more tense as the new year progressed. There were taunts and scuffles in the streets; political divisions were becoming more sharply drawn by the day; the middle ground grew harder to hold so that even those who did not want to choose sides were being forced to do so. There was little way for the British command to present what was happening in a good light. More and more it seemed the British were prisoners in, rather than occupiers of, Boston.

The twins, Justin, and Silas watched in sorrow as Marcus became more outspokenly Tory by the day, placing himself among those who urged General Gage to more decisive action against their rebellious fellow citizens. Marcus was increasingly afraid of the "rabble" and what they might do to the ordered, prosperous life he had worked so diligently to establish. Over Justin's protests, he ordered that the paper no longer print material with Whig sentiments.

"You will take much of the life from it. And, worse, you endanger yourself by attracting the attention of the radicals." *Including some who are close friends of mine*, Justin added silently as he argued with his father.

But Marcus would have none of it. "I am the King's man. I have made no secret of this. Nor am I ashamed of it. Things have come to such a pass, I will not encourage those radicals further by printing their treasonous filth."

There was no use in continued discussion, and Justin knew he would have to try to make excuses to Dr. Joseph Warren, who as a member of the Massachusetts Committee of Safety was the most powerful Whig in Boston and in the Sons of Liberty. Not all of the Sons of

Liberty were as reasonable as Mr. Revere and Dr. Church. He didn't want any mysterious night fires, particularly with Silas living above the printing office and Ad next door. The Sons of Liberty would have to remember that no matter how offensive the newspaper's contents, the same business produced some of the broadsides that appeared all over town under cover of darkness. And he and Silas would have to continue to alter the books and the inventory list to keep producing the broadsides. He felt more than a little guilt, and not only about stealing from the printing office and thus from his father, who trusted them all so much that he spent less and less time at the shops. Now it was Ad and Silas who ran off the broadsides at night, risking discovery. Justin tried to be there when he could, but it was different, being married.

Now he understood Addie's puzzlement when he had tried to explain that Sarah had little interest in politics. Sarah was very much interested in his company and his safety, and thus she was becoming interested in politics as well. She didn't pout or protest when he went out at night, she just looked so sad he could scarcely bear it.

"You know there is no other woman?" he asked her anxiously.

"I know that," she answered, "but perhaps a woman would be an easier rival than politics." At his look of surprise, she smiled dolefully. "Justin, do you think me such a silly, shallow creature that I don't know where your loyalty lies? Do you think I haven't suspected for a long while that you're involved with the Sons of Liberty?"

Her words made him feel as if all the air had been knocked from his lungs. He tried to speak, shook his head and tried again. "Great God! I hope I am not so transparent to others as I am to you!"

"I hope not, too, for those others would be seeing you with eyes of love as I do, and then I would be jealous. I see the fire in your eyes when you speak of justice, of an Englishman's rights, of what is owed the King and what is not." This much she would say, but her deepest secret she would not reveal to him. She was not joking about her political rival. She was desperately jealous of that passion in him and fearful of the risks he was willing to take for his beliefs. She was coming to understand that an idea could be the most demanding and pitiless of all mistresses. And she understood that the only way she could fight this foe was to provide Justin with the human warmth and welcome an idea could not give. Out of necessity, she was developing more interest in politics because in her heart she knew she could not be first in Justin's affections until settlement was reached with the mother country. Her worst nightmare was that open warfare might come before a settlement.

For his part, Justin was discovering that Sarah was much more complex than he had known during their courtship. He had thought her beautiful and desirable from the day he'd first met her in the bookstore, where she had been perusing the latest novels from England, and as he'd gotten to know her, his practical side had decided she would make a very suitable wife. Now he was surprised and delighted daily by the unexpected depths of her heart and mind. But he was also finding sorrow in the knowledge that unlike Marcus, Sarah's father had not deemed it necessary to have his daughter educated beyond the basics thought sufficient for a girl, this despite Sarah being their only living child and beloved of her parents. It touched him to see her struggling to read and comprehend the political essays he found so fascinating.

One evening he was distracted from his reading by watching Sarah's efforts. She was reading John Locke's *Two Treatises of Government*, her mouth shaping each word silently as she read, a frown of concentration puckering her forehead. Justin saw the soft candlelight shimmering in her golden hair, and then he noticed that the light was also catching in her tears.

She looked at him, and the tears overflowed. "I am so ignorant, so stupid! In one second I think I understand and in the next it doesn't even seem to be in English! You will grow bored with me, you will! You know so much, and I know so little!" she sobbed.

Justin picked her up and settled down again with her in his lap, her skirt and petticoats billowing and settling around both of them. She was so startled, her tears stopped.

"That's better," Justin said, nuzzling her neck, but he ignored his rising desire and chose his words carefully. "I cannot bear to see you cry, particularly over this. You are not stupid! You are simply untutored. You can learn anything you want to learn, but you need not do it for me. I love you as you are, wise and beautiful. If you want to know more than you do, then you will learn it. And when we have daughters, we will make sure they are educated as well as our sons."

"Then I will have to study diligently so that our children won't find me wanting." Determination was replacing Sarah's distress, and she savored the thought of children to come and years to share them with Justin.

She giggled when he yawned elaborately.

"Wife, I think it is time we retired for the night. It's chilly here, and I can think of ways to warm us up."

Sarah shivered not with the chill but with anticipation, and when they were in bed with the hangings drawn against the draft, she was as greedy for his touch as he for hers. She tested the sleekness of his body with her hands and answered the urgency of his mouth. They came together with the joyful abandon of two healthy young animals, and for a few hours they blocked out the hazards of the future with lovemaking and sleep.

But Sarah was thinking of the future when she called on Addie the next day.

Addie liked her sister-in-law well enough, but they were not close friends. She was apprehensive about Sarah coming to visit her because she seemed nervous, her fingers pleating, the heavy wool of her dress worn against the cold of a snowy day. Addie feared Sarah had come to her with some complaint against Justin, and she was ready to say she would not get involved in any way in her brother's marriage.

Sarah declined any refreshment as her fingers continued their agitated dance. She drew a deep breath and announced, "I want to learn to read French and Latin and Greek. I want to learn to understand more of what interests Justin and the rest of you. I want you to teach me, if you will."

Addie was so stunned, she could only stare while she tried to gather her wits. "Did Justin? Does Justin?"

"Justin says he loves me as I am," Sarah stated firmly. "But I don't. Any small child in a dame school knows as much and probably more than I. I want to know more for myself as much as for Justin."

Sarah looked so resolute and hopeful, all the objections Addie could think of faded before she gave them voice, and she heard herself saying, "I would be glad to tutor you."

She was rewarded by Sarah's brilliant smile. "If it doesn't make you uncomfortable, I would prefer we not tell Justin. He might find out anyway, but if not, I would like to surprise him. We could pretend our visits are social."

That was acceptable to Addie because if Sarah proved a bad pupil, it would be better she not be further crushed by Justin knowing.

Addie took the project on only to help Sarah and, indirectly, Justin, but charitable motives were soon beside the point. Sarah was a clever pupil. It was as if her mind had been starving for years. She was so eager for knowledge, it was usually Addie who tired first. And she didn't learn by rote; she juggled ideas like bright golden balls, making them into this pattern and that, trying to understand all the designs, trying to understand, above all, how Justin had formed his political beliefs.

"If it is true that men have the right to determine how they will be governed and that they owe no allegiance to the kings above them unless by their consent, then what prevents all of society from falling into chaos?" She blushed and ducked her head. "Perhaps I have missed something, and this is a foolish question."

Addie grinned at her. "It is not foolish! It is exactly what the great minds of our age are asking. And no one seems to have the answer yet."

Though it was a serious topic, Sarah looked so pleased with herself, Addie couldn't help but share her pleasure.

She began to share other things with Sarah. Addie had such close relationships with Ad and Justin, she had never felt the lack of intimate female friends. Sissy was special to her, but she lived far away and now her letters were filled with paeans to the bliss of married life, which only made Addie wish Silas were not continuing to behave with such admirable, to his mind, restraint. Addie found Sarah was a good listener and willing to be a good friend. It was easier by the day to understand why Justin had married her.

By unspoken consent, they did not discuss Justin, Silas, and Ad's involvement with the Sons of Liberty. It was dangerous to speak of it, and it was futile because neither Sarah nor Addie knew exactly what the young men were doing. But there was increasingly less inhibition about other topics.

"He says it will not happen, but I fear I will bore Justin one day," Sarah confided. "My looks are ordinary, and they will fade. That is why I must become an interesting woman."

Though her coloring was similar to Sissy's, Sarah was so small and exquisitely made, Sissy would appear robust beside her, and Addie felt like a veritable giantess in comparison to her sister-in-law. She regarded her with amazement. "But you are beautiful, anything but ordinary, and I know my brother finds you most interesting."

Sarah grimaced. "I thank you for the compliments, but blond hair and blue eyes are ordinary, not at all like you, Ad, and Justin. You are so striking, people are compelled to look at you, including the redcoats who visit here. But they hardly signify, do they, when you care so much for Silas Bradwell? You needn't be so surprised that I know; it's quite evident. What I don't understand is why he's being so distant."

Addie felt as if an enormous burden had been lifted from her. At last she had someone she could talk to, and the words poured out as she told Sarah everything, even about how she had dreamed of Silas while she was in Virginia, even about his kiss and his confession of love.

"I would marry him today, but his damnable sense of honor hardly allows him to spend a minute in my company, let alone anything more serious."

"Would you love him so much were he different, less honorable?" Sarah asked. "By the normal measure of such things, he is not worthy to marry you." She held her hand up to stay Addie's protest. "I am not saying he is not, for I believe that no more than you do. But he believes it, and that is the important thing. Surely you can see it through his eyes. He was rescued by your father. He feels he owes all to him. I doubt it occurs to him that he has given your father not only years of good work but also what must be pleasure in aiding the transformation of a homeless urchin into a fine man. And this present business"—her voice dropped so low, Addie had to strain to hear her—"must be even more difficult for Silas than for your brothers. Justin and Ad belong to your father by blood, no matter what happens. Silas does not. He undoubtedly believes he belongs only by his gratitude to your father for his charity. With charity at one end and gratitude at the other, what an awful chain that must be."

So eloquently did Sarah argue Silas's case, Addie had the eerie sense that he was there in place of Justin's petite wife.

"You may have only a beginner's knowledge of the classics, but you know much about the human heart. I will teach you what you wish to know from books, and you will teach me patience and understanding."

Sarah did more than that. She frequently invited the twins and Silas to dine with her and Justin, though Ad usually made some excuse because he didn't want to distract Addie and Silas's attention from each other. Sarah pretended her sole motivation was to share the pride she had in her newly formed household.

Silas could not withstand her soft persuasion, and he didn't wish to. When he was with the little group, he could pretend that he and Addie were no different from Justin and Sarah.

Addie didn't have to pretend. As far as she was concerned, they were like the other couple—suited for each other, in love with each other. She must only persevere until Silas realized it. She paid far more heed than ever before to her appearance, fussing until Tullia observed with a chuckle, "My little girl is growing up, but it sure is taking a deal of work."

Addie was working at more than how she looked; she was learning step by step how to tempt Silas. When she put her hand on his arm, she could feel his muscles tense under the fabric of his coat and shirt. When she looked at him a certain way, Silas would forget what he was saying. When he escorted her home from Justin and Sarah's house, she seized every excuse to cuddle as close to him as possible, as if she feared the hazards of the street. She went so far as to make sure she was not so encumbered by hoops and petticoats that too much distance might be put between them.

Finally, one evening, he lost his temper. He pulled her into an empty doorway and gave her a little shake. "You are driving me mad, and you are doing it deliberately! You trust me too far." His mouth came down on hers, hard and punishing for the frustration she was causing him, warning her off. But she didn't regard the warning. She was inexperienced, not unwilling, and she met his kiss with her own need, accepting his anger until it gentled and she tasted his mouth and tested the firm texture of it. The kiss was flavored with the spiced cider they had drunk, and Addie learned how erotic apples and cinnamon and cloves could be.

It was Silas who broke the kiss and stood trembling, his head bowed as he fought for control. "You play with fire!" His voice grated.

"I am not playing. I love you. I want to be married to you. I want to share your days and your nights. And I don't give a damn what Parliament or the Congress decides to do; neither should have a bloody thing to do with our marriage!"

Silas was shocked, having never before heard Addie speak so vulgarly, and then he was amused enough to laugh. He cradled her against him, and she could feel the laughter vibrating in his chest. "I expect you will still surprise me when you're an old woman and I an old man. I—"

Whatever else he was going to say was lost as four soldiers spotted them.

"Who goes there?" The soldier who called out sounded as frightened as he was challenging.

Then another said, "'Tis only a couple courting. They must not 'ave a room a their own."

Silas bristled at the insolent tone, but Addie gripped his hand firmly and said, "By your leave, gentlemen, we will be on our way."

Her educated speech made the soldiers uneasy, and one of them muttered, "Well, go along then."

Addie pulled Silas into motion. Her heart was pounding with fear that he might berate the soldiers.

"I am angry, but I am not a fool," he said when they were safely away from the redcoats. He didn't sound angry; he sounded weary, resigned, and totally devoid of his earlier passion.

When he left her at the house, he did not kiss her; he touched her cheek briefly and was gone. Inwardly she cursed their encounter with the redcoats; it had reminded Silas of the power of the occupying army and of his powerlessness. Though Addie had spoken to the soldiers to protect Silas, she was sorry she had. She'd not meant to make him feel inadequate.

Patience, she reminded herself. Silas was worth endless patience.

She was nearly to the door of her bedchamber upstairs when she heard the music coming from Quentin's room. She felt a pang of guilt. He was so undemanding, so intent on his pursuits, it was easy to neglect him. He had resumed his studies with a tutor since returning from Virginia, but if things were normal, he would have been off at college in the company of other young men.

Addie froze in the act of knocking on his door. She recognized the riffles of sound he was creating and the instrument he was playing. They were military airs played on a fife, which, accompanied by the beat of a drum, could guide troop movements in the thunder of battle when the high notes of the fife could be heard above the guns and the low vibrations of the drums could be heard below.

The music stopped abruptly when Addie knocked, but when she entered, Quentin smiled at her in his typical, slightly distracted fashion, as if there was nothing unusual in his playing music composed to send men to death.

"Why are you practicing this… this…"

"It's music, Addie, even if it is used to set soldiers marching," Quentin pointed out coolly, but there was a stubborn set to his jaw that warned her this was not a subject he was going to discuss very far with her.

She looked at Quentin, really looked at him and saw that while he was not yet a man, he was no longer a child in this his fifteenth year. She wanted to scream at him that she couldn't bear it if he got involved in the current troubles as their brothers and Silas were. But it would do no good. No one had ever changed Quentin's mind about anything once he had set his course.

She turned away without another word, afraid she would cry in front of him. She heard his voice following her out of the room.

"Don't worry, Addie. This music is just something more to know."

Once in the sanctuary of her room, she let the tears fall. Word was coming from England that the various petitions and declarations from the Congress were being met with hostility rather than sympathy. She tried to find reason to hope, but it was difficult. Marking the anniversary of the Boston Massacre had caused a near riot, with Dr. Warren having to crawl through a window of Old South in order to address the crowd, and redcoats swarming in to jam the steps to the pulpit and threaten Dr. Warren's life. Bloodshed had been very near. It did not seem possible that things could go on indefinitely as they were.

Her fear was realized in the early days of April. The redcoats didn't come to visit so often, and when they did they were more on edge, less open than they had been. Marcus behaved in an opposite fashion, looking happier than he had in months, and in the company of other Loyalists, he called on General Gage several times.

Addie reported everything to Silas, Justin, and Ad.

"It's not much of a secret," Justin told her. "General Gage is planning something, probably a raid on military stores again. The questions are where he will try to strike, when, and how he will move the troops from the town."

"He has but two choices regarding troop movements," Silas said. "He can either march them across the Neck or load them in boats and go by water. It's impossible to predict which he will do when we do not know his target. So we watch."

It wasn't long before they and others noted that longboats from British naval vessels were being run out and refurbished. Word went out to nearby towns from the Provincial Congress, which was meeting in Concord in defiance of the British government, to be alert to British troops by land or sea.

The Provincial Congress was to adjourn on April 15 so that delegates chosen for the Second Continental Congress would have time to travel to Philadelphia for the session to begin in May. The delegates seemed as likely a target as munitions, since the capture of the Massachusetts leaders would be a grand stroke for the British authorities. But if that were the plan, it would have to be carried out swiftly before the delegates departed southward.

Silas avoided Addie, Justin snapped at Sarah, and Ad would not have admitted his apprehension to anyone. They patrolled Boston's streets for longer hours than before, dodging soldiers, waiting cold, weary hours to discover any stealthy troop movements that might be cloaked by the dark, and watching no less closely during the day.

The grenadier and light infantry companies, the most mobile British troops, of every regiment had been relieved of garrison duties. These companies were directed to new exercises and to keep themselves in a state of readiness. Boston was too small a town for these major changes to go unremarked. And it was logical to assume that these were the troops that would be employed on whatever raid was being planned.

April 16 was Easter Sunday. At Addie's insistence, her brothers, Sarah, and Silas attended church services with Marcus and the rest of the family.

"It may be the last time we are all together," Addie had told the men. "I know you don't want to worship in a nest of Tories, but do it for Papa. Allow him to believe that all is well for just a little longer."

Despite being surrounded by a sea of redcoats, they tolerated the service at King's Chapel, but that did not prevent them from noticing that in the harbor, longboats were being secured to the sterns of warships.

The young men made themselves endure Sunday dinner as if nothing were out of the ordinary, but Justin suffered a terrible yearning to turn back the clock to the time before his path and his father's had diverged. He wanted to put his arms around Marcus, to thank him, to tell him openly of his love and respect. Instead, he bounced little Clement on his knee.

"He looks like you, Papa. With you and Mary to raise him, he will be a fine man."

Marcus regarded him intently, as if he heard what Justin longed to say, but then he simply smiled. "Of course he will be, and I expect all of his brothers and sisters to help make him so."

Addie heard the words Justin did not say and felt the pain in the silence. But she was comforted as she met first Sarah's eyes and then

Mary's. They had heard as clearly as she, and to share the sorrow made it easier.

But still, it was hard to see the young men leave the house, and she envied Sarah for being able to go with Justin, to be with him for a while longer. She wished she were leaving with Silas, but he bid her good day as if this were just an ordinary Sunday.

Sunday night passed without incident, but the longboats remained in evidence, and there was no relaxation of the tension that gripped the troops in Boston.

Sarah spent much of Monday with Addie, but for all their efforts to distract themselves, they made little progress with Sarah's studies, passing the time in long silences punctuated by futile speculation.

"Mayhap nothing much will come of this even if the soldiers do go raiding, for they have gone out before," Sarah suggested.

"It is different now," Addie pointed out reluctantly. "Tempers are higher than ever, and the militia is ready to rise from every town and farm."

"If only General Gage will keep his men in Boston until—"

"Until what? Until Parliament and the King's ministers change their minds? Or until men like my brothers change theirs?" Despair washed over Addie.

But the redcoats stayed in the town through that day and night and the following day, so that by Tuesday evening, Justin, Ad, and Silas were tempted to consider that Gage had cancelled whatever plans he had made.

"I don't know whether I'll be relieved if that is true," Silas confessed. "This hellish waiting almost makes me wish something would happen."

Not many hours later, though he knew he was being foolishly superstitious, he felt guilty for having spoken the wish aloud, no matter how tentative.

Word spread like fire through the network of spies that the British were moving tonight. One of the first confirmations came from a Mistress Stedman. She employed the wife of a British grenadier named Gibson, and despite her Whig convictions, she was fond of the couple. That evening, a fully uniformed grenadier had knocked at Mistress Stedman's door and had inquired after Gibson. When told that Gibson was not there, the grenadier had left word that he was to report at eight o'clock at the bottom of the Common. He was to be in full field dress and ready to march.

Mistress Stedman wasted no time in reporting to her husband, who passed the word to Dr. Church, who in turn sent the information racing through the ranks of the Sons of Liberty and other supporters. Most importantly, the information went to Dr. Warren who continued to act as Patriot leader in Boston. Dr. Warren had had numerous reports that the British troops would march in darkness. And now this summons for the troops to gather at the bottom of the Common gave every indication that the longboats were going to be put to use.

Justin, Silas, and Ad did not question Dr. Warren's orders. He was an engaging, intelligent man whose air of confidence inspired the same in them. They willingly carried messages and ran errands from Dr. Warren's house on Hanover Street, all the while keeping watch for British patrols.

Dr. Warren had directed a courier to leave Boston for Lexington and Concord at nightfall by way of the Neck and to warn people along the route that the redcoats might be heading their way to capture military stores there. He sent Justin and Silas to summon Mr. Revere while Ad slipped away to make sure that the boat Revere had kept secreted for a year for just this purpose was still in its hiding place.

When they rendezvoused with Ad, he confirmed that Revere and two friends had taken the boat. "I wish I could have gone with them, but they didn't need me."

"Each of us has done what we were ordered to do," Justin reminded him. "We couldn't have done better than that."

They and the others spread throughout the town had been far more efficient than the British. The expeditionary force had been loaded and ferried slowly across to the shore near Cambridge. If General Gage had believed such a large movement of troops could be kept secret, he was badly mistaken. Many watchers heard the hushed voices, the creak of equipment, the shuffle of feet.

"There's nothing more we can do tonight," Justin said. "I'm going home to Sarah, and I suggest both of you also seek your beds."

Ad was weary and sleep beckoned, but he wished he could discuss the night's events with Addie. While he appreciated the independence of living in his own quarters, he missed the old closeness of mind he had shared with his twin.

Silas missed Addie, too, for different reasons. He envied Justin more tonight than ever before. He wished he were going home to a wife, to Addie. He wished he could hold her through what remained of the night and have her beside him to face whatever tomorrow would bring. And the worst of it was that he alone was responsible for his loneliness.

The next morning dawned damp and chill and was not far advanced before most of the town knew that redcoats were out in the countryside, but few knew if anything else had happened.

What had happened was that Revere had used his boat to cross to the Charlestown shore, and went by horse from there to spread the warning. He was the obvious choice for this mission. It wasn't the first time he had carried important news. The morning after the Tea Party, Samuel Adams had sent him to carry the news to New York and Philadelphia. The next year he had ridden to Philadelphia again, making the trip in five days to rush the Suffolk Resolves to the Congress. And the past December he had raced to Portsmouth, New Hampshire, carrying word that Parliament had acted to cut off shipments of arms and ammunition. Patriots there had promptly seized powder from the King's fort.

Mr. Revere's house was on North Square, and though the square was open again, earlier in the evening soldiers had blocked it off. Many redcoats were billeted in and around the square, and it was plain that the evening's flurry of activity had had to do with the muster on the Common. But since the soldiers had pretended nothing special was happening, civilians likewise had carried on as if naught was amiss, and Justin and Silas had not been stopped. They had returned to Dr. Warren's with Revere, and Dr. Warren had directed him to row to Charlestown and spread the word that the British were embarking.

"It is supposed they are going to Lexington, by way of Watertown, to take Messieurs Adams and Hancock, and to go on to Concord," said Dr. Warren.

Justin heard Silas's sharp intake of breath beside him, and his own heart jumped. Samuel Adams and John Hancock were too important to their cause to lose, and it was a shock to hear Dr. Warren confirming the rumor that the British intended to do more than capture armaments.

Warren told Revere, "Ad would have reported back to us if there was trouble with your boat. He has not done so. He will be keeping watch there. Godspeed to you."

Revere nodded and took his leave as calmly as if he were going for a pleasurable outing rather than trying to row undetected past a British man-of-war.

"There is one more task, and then we will have done all we can from here to tell our friends what is happening this night."

Dr. Warren had then sent Justin and Silas on their way in the company of a militia captain, and in spite of the danger of what they were doing, they had found a certain ironic pleasure in their business being at Christ Church.

Christ Church was Anglican, the second one built in Boston, after King's Chapel, and it had a long history of association with influential families who were dedicated adherents of the Crown, Sarah's parents among them. But the church sexton was a friend of Revere, and had allowed the captain to climb up and place two lanterns in the church's tower while Justin and Silas kept watch. It was an agreed-upon signal to warn their supporters in Charlestown that the British were leaving by water.

The moon had been rising and was nearly full, but due to an odd, low declination, it had not illuminated the waters where Revere was rowing. Justin and Silas had heard no boom of guns or shouts of alarm across the water, and they'd had to trust that, with the help of the heavens, Revere's mission had been succeeding. And also that, because of the lanterns' signal, watchers in Charlestown had known what was happening before Revere landed on their shore, and helped spread the word.

One who did know what had happened since Revere had crossed the water was Dr. Warren. That next morning, Silas, Justin, and Ad presented themselves at his house early enough to get the news when he did that there had been a clash of arms at the village of Lexington, and he was blunt in telling them he was leaving the city to join the militia, though he did not press them to go with him. They had often discussed the possibility of having to quit the town at a moment's notice, but planning it and doing it were very different.

"If the militia are fighting, they will need every man," Silas said.

"And the sooner the better," Justin agreed.

"But without telling Addie or anyone at home?" Ad's voice cracked.

"Meet me at my house. I'll tell Sarah. She will tell Addie. Addie will have to tell Papa if we're not back by tomorrow morning. God forgive me for being such a coward. We don't have time to waste." Justin's own voice wasn't altogether steady when he spoke of their father.

He returned to his home while Silas and Ad went to their rooms to gather essentials, choosing carefully because to be too burdened would cause suspicion. Ad left from his quarters above the bookstore and Silas from his above the printing office, and neither of them said anything to the printer's devil or to the clerks. This was particularly hard for Silas. Marcus trusted him as much as he trusted his sons, and now the three of them were abandoning the businesses Marcus had worked so hard to establish. The other workers were trustworthy, but it was not the same. Silas knew he was betraying one obligation of honor to fulfill another. And he was leaving Addie. He could not think about that.

Sarah took one look at Justin's face, and her own went bone white. He put his arms around her.

"It's started. We've got reports that the militia have taken on the redcoats. I don't know anything more except that I have to go. Silas and Ad, too. Perhaps it will come to nothing, and we will be back by tonight or by tomorrow morning. But if not, I'll send word as soon as I can." He could feel her beginning to tremble in his arms. "I'm sorry, my love, but I have no choice. I must go. And I have to ask you to tell Addie."

He tipped her face up and wiped gently at the tears that were beginning to overflow. "I know how much I am asking of you, so much. I love you, and I don't want to leave you."

He could see her gathering her strength.

"I will tell Addie, and I will wait for you to come back, whenever that will be." And then she added very softly, "Je t'aime."

At his look of startled inquiry, she managed a smile. "Shall I tell you I love you in Latin and in Greek as well? I have been studying with Addie. I meant to know much, much more before I told you. I meant it to be a surprise. I mean to be an interesting woman so you will never regret marrying me." Her lips were quivering so badly, she put her hand against them.

"Oh, Sarah, it is a surprise, and your effort is a magnificent gift, but I need no changes in you. I will never regret marrying you, never!" Justin's eyes filled with tears. He pulled her hand away from her mouth and kissed her. "Damn, there is no time! Help me collect a few things, please."

Sarah squared her shoulders and was far more efficient than he. And not only did she insist he take all the money they had in the house, she also demanded he pack the spoons from their silver service. "If you don't need them, you can bring them back when you return to me. But I want to know you will have the silver to buy what you need."

"This may yet prove a false alarm. We might be back before the sun sets."

"Then I shall put the spoons back in their places." Sarah's words were all practicality, but her eyes reflected her fear and love.

Silas and Ad appeared, and there was no more time. She kept her smile in place and watched from the doorway until they were out of sight. She allowed only a few more tears to escape before she wiped them away impatiently and set out to visit Addie.

Chapter 7

Justin, Silas, and Ad crossed by ferry to Charlestown and were on their way to Lexington when their way was blocked by redcoats guarding a baggage train.

Silas saw Ad's hand drifting toward the pistol he had concealed beneath his coat. "Don't do it!" he hissed. "Don't provoke them. There are too many of them."

But Silas, too, found it difficult to wait calmly as two British officers rode up to them, and then he listened incredulously as the officers asked if they had seen the main body of Lord Percy's force. This was the baggage train belonging to that force.

They were able to answer honestly that they had not, and to their surprised relief, the officers allowed them to go on.

"They must be in great confusion to let us pass," Justin said.

"Or else they see no threat from provincials," Silas suggested.

As they proceeded on their way, they were aided by a merchant, who after questioning them sharply, took them up in his carriage. He had no intention of joining the fray himself, but he wanted the redcoats to be taught a lesson. On the journey, they gleaned a clearer picture of what was happening as they saw militia streaming toward the scene of action. The British forces were confused, but the Patriots were not. They, with their vast network of watchers and messengers, now knew exactly what was going on.

British troops had marched out of Boston over the Neck that morning, but due to delays in the city, this relief column was late in supporting the men who had left the town by longboat the night before. Those troops had landed in a swampy area near Cambridge, most of them getting wet to their knees. Then they had waited for food distribution before moving out, only to cross a ford that drenched them to the waists in icy water. But they had gotten to Lexington in the early hours of the morning, and they had easily defeated the little group of minutemen who had turned out to obstruct their way.

There were conflicting accounts of which side had fired first, but once those first shots were loosed, the British had laid down a deadly volley that had killed at least ten and wounded another nine or so. The numbers didn't matter as much as the fact that armed conflict had begun.

The goal of the British raid was the cannon at Concord, and after Lexington the soldiers marched on. But even before the first shot had been fired at Lexington, other minutemen had been gathering their weapons as word spread that the British were out. Farmers abandoned their fields, merchants their shops, teachers their classrooms, on and on, to head toward Concord as quickly as they could. By the time the British arrived, the local militia had been reinforced by men from neighboring towns. The redcoats found they had tarried too long and had underestimated both the ability and the willingness of the populace to turn out against them.

Justin, Ad, and Silas were among the reinforcements who joined the minutemen at Meriam's Corner, a mile east of Concord, where some British soldiers were retreating after their failed attempts in Concord. The young men had spoken about armed conflict, had trained for it, but nothing had prepared them for the reality.

The British made wonderful targets, marching down the road in bright-red coats with buckles and blades glinting in the sun. In contrast, the Americans fired from behind stone walls, trees, hedges, and houses, making it difficult for the enemy to see them, let alone shoot them.

Ad couldn't shake the feeling that it was all a game. Even with the sound of muskets and pistols firing all around him and the smoke of gunpowder filling his eyes and nose, even with the cries of men, it did not seem real, not until he aimed his pistol and fired. He saw his mark as if down a long tunnel with nothing else in the universe except himself and the soldier he had chosen. It was as if he could see the ball flying toward the man, as if he felt its impact in his own chest. He saw blood blossom dark on the red coat, bright on the white facings. He saw the man stagger and fall, saw two of his comrades lift him, one under each arm to carry him along with them. He saw the wounded man's face in a clear, brief flash, and he thought perhaps he had seen the soldier at the Valencourt house, attending an officer.

"God, I hit him," he groaned. He fell to his knees and retched violently behind the stone wall as the sickness slammed into him. He was far more ashamed of what he had done than he was of being on his knees vomiting like a puling infant.

"I feel as you do," Justin told him, "but instead of a heaving stomach, I've got Tullia's beef jelly for knees."

Silas was more to the point. "You can go back to Boston and pretend that none of this happened. The British are in such disarray, they could never know you came out today. Go back, take the ferry from Charlestown and then you can think about what you want to do next. Neither your brother nor I will think badly of you, and Addie's joy will be boundless."

Ad wiped his mouth and got to his feet. "I would think badly of myself. I am recovered now. For a moment, I forgot that they killed some of ours this morning and will kill as many more as they can."

As they hurried to catch up with the main body of the militia, Justin thought he had just seen the last of Ad's childhood vanish in a brief instant, and Silas wished Ad had gone back to Boston for Addie's sake. And not for anything would Silas have admitted that he felt physically sick, too, and wanted more than anything to be back at the printing office with the chance that he might catch a glimpse of Addie before the day was over.

The British soldiers in the retreating brigade, commanded by Colonel Smith, were in sorry shape when they reached Lexington. It was obvious that months of limited activity in Boston had left them unprepared for the rigors of this day. However, in Lexington, they met with the relief force under Brigadier General Lord Percy, who, having had reports of events in Concord, had formed his troops on Lexington Common, with a couple of artillery pieces loaded with grapeshot and canister to use against the colonists. The union of the two forces gave the British a better chance of getting back to Boston, but they could not leave until the men had rested.

Lord Percy was in command when the British began their retreat from Lexington, heading for Cambridge. They were orderly at first, but the Patriots continued to fire on them from every side, from behind every form of cover they could find, and gradually, the discipline of the British began to break down.

As he did his best to kill redcoats and keep his own hide intact, Silas watched, with a kind of detached pity, the enemy's deterioration. The soldiers' faces were begrimed, and sweat stained their heavy uniforms. Some of their faces were so red, it was a wonder they did not collapse of ruptured blood vessels. They choked on the clouds of dust raised by their feet. Their tight formation began to come apart as parties broke off to dash out against the Patriots, as if the redcoats were being driven mad by the attacks coming from all sides. Then, to his utter amazement, Silas noticed that some soldiers seemed to be going after plunder in houses along the way.

"Don't they know they're retreating?" Justin said as he noted the same thing.

Ad made no comment. His first taste of war had already taught him it was an insane enterprise. It didn't seem strange to him that everything made sense because nothing did. It did not even seem odd to him when he realized there were women among the Patriots, firing on the soldiers as steadily as the men. Ad gave thanks that Addie wasn't with them. She was a fine shot, but for him, that would have been the final madness of the day.

The redcoats who charged the Patriots and those who separated from the main body to pillage created additional havoc, but they also became more vulnerable to attack themselves. And as word passed that the British were killing unarmed civilians along the way, word underscored by the smoke and flames rising from some buildings, rage against the soldiers boiled high.

Justin spotted smoke beginning to seep from a farmhouse a short distance away, and though he knew they would probably be too late, he started to run with Silas and Ad close on his heels. They skidded to a stop and ducked behind an outbuilding as four redcoats staggered out of the house, loaded down with plunder.

"Lay down your arms," Justin shouted. "We have you surrounded."

"What will we do with four prisoners?" Silas muttered, but the redcoats did not intend to be taken. Their booty went flying as they shouldered their weapons and swung the long muzzles of their muskets toward Justin's voice.

"They haven't the sense to seek cover," Ad said under his breath just before the first shot was fired at their hiding place.

But the shot was wide, and it was apparent that the soldiers hadn't been staggering only because of the goods they'd been carrying; they had also consumed enough of some spirit, probably rum, to be very drunk. The man who had fired his weapon didn't bother reloading.

"Hell, I don't want to shoot drunken men," Silas swore, but in the next instant, everything changed as they heard a piercing scream and saw a woman clutching the frame of the front door as more smoke billowed from the house.

One of the soldiers turned on the woman. Justin took aim and fired, hitting the man in the back. The woman screamed again as the soldier fell to his knees and toppled face down into the dirt. Justin was reloading his weapon before the soldier had finished falling.

"We rush them now?" he asked, and Silas and Ad nodded.

They sprang from cover and ran straight at the soldiers, yelling at the top of their lungs. Two of the soldiers still had loaded muskets, but they were so startled at being charged, they fired wildly. One of the shots went through Silas's coat while the other went wide, and then the two groups of men collided. It could hardly be called a fight. The redcoats were too drunk and too dazed by the onslaught of the Americans and the wounding of one of their own to offer effective resistance.

"Get the woman away from the house," Justin told Ad once they had the three subdued. The fourth soldier, the one he had shot, hadn't moved since he'd fallen.

Ad could see flames spreading through the house and could feel the heat as he went to the woman who still clung to the door frame. "Come on now, ma'am. It isn't safe for you to stay here." He was shocked to see how young she appeared and that she was heavy with child.

He offered his arm gingerly, expecting she would collapse in hysterics at any moment. Instead, she straightened her spine and went with him after one sad look back at the burning house. When she looked at the redcoats, her face contorted with rage, and she spat on one of them. "I wish you would kill them all," she said. "I wish I had the courage to do it myself." And then she turned her back on the soldiers.

Though they had no orders regarding prisoners and taking these men with them would only slow them down, they didn't have the stomach for execution and went so far as to drag the soldiers farther from the fire before stripping them of their weapons and trussing them securely. Silas doubted the wounded man was still alive, but he tied him up as if he were, thinking that would be easier for Justin. It would be hard enough for Justin that he had shot a man in the back without learning he had killed him.

"I'm sorry, there's nothing we can do to save your house, and we must go on. More redcoats might come. Where can we escort you to safety?" Silas asked the woman.

She would have preferred they return to the fight right away, since her husband was with the militia and she wanted him to have every advantage. But she agreed to let them take her to a neighboring farm farther back from the road and so less likely to be invaded by the enemy. At the neighbor's house the three men were given cold spring water to drink and food to take with them.

The entire incident had taken little time, but it seemed to have been hours. It made them aware of what it was going to be like to fight on their own ground in a civil war with Englishmen on both sides and civilians caught in the middle.

The longboats that had brought Smith's men across from Boston would not be enough to take the combined forces back, even if the boats could reach them. And the route Percy's force had used that morning included a bridge over the Charles River between Cambridge and Brighton, a bridge they assumed now destroyed. It was foolhardy for them to assume otherwise, with the Patriots bent on impeding every step of their progress. In a day filled with bad decisions, Lord Percy, now in command of the whole operation, seemed to be acting wisely despite his precarious position.

The British thus headed for Charlestown and the causeway that connected the peninsula to the mainland. Justin, Silas, and Ad rushed with a large body of militia to attack the redcoats before they got across. Ahead of them, and close on the heels of the British, was a large body of men from Salem and Marblehead. But Lord Percy held steady, getting his men across just ahead of the militia and back within the range of the guns of their fleet.

The British were exhausted, battered, and they had had to retreat from the provincials they held in such contempt. But they had escaped the humiliation of total defeat and capture. Still, there was proof now that the British were prisoners in Boston, not a conquering army that could attack at will.

Ad gazed around at the milling knots of militia. He felt more numb than anything else, and he saw the same dullness in the others' eyes. "What do we do now?"

Most of the minutemen could return to their homes, but no one knew what the British intended to do next. They had to be watched.

Justin, Ad, and Silas had friends outside of Boston, people they could stay with, and they knew they could also find shelter and ample food at Mary's farm. But Boston was home, and the people they loved were there. It was such a short distance away, but it might as well have been across the sea.

"I told Sarah we might be home by nightfall," Justin said softly. "Though she made me take our silver spoons."

"Addie is going to have a bad time telling your father where we've gone," Silas said.

"Do you think he will ever speak to us again?" Ad asked.

They had no answer for that, and though they had spent the day fighting and killing, it was as if time had slipped its moorings and they were three young boys who had gone off on an adventure and now wanted nothing more than to go home.

Silas rubbed a hand over his face, feeling grit and stubble on his skin. "There is nothing more we can do this day except find food and shelter. Perhaps things will be more plain on the morrow."

He doubted that, but he was resolved that he would ease the way as much as he could for Justin and Ad. He not only loved them as brothers, it was also the least he could do for Marcus. Ad's question repeated itself over and over in his mind. Whatever Marcus decided about his sons, Silas was sure he himself would never be forgiven. The loss was a deep ache inside of him made much, much worse by the knowledge that he was further than ever from being able to marry Addie. For a moment, she so filled his mind it was as if she were standing before him. The vision faded, and he trudged down the road with Justin and Ad.

Chapter 8

By the time Sarah got across town to the house on Summer Street, she knew that in addition to the troops that had left the night before, more were mustering to march out of the city by way of the Neck. News was not difficult to gather, nor were rumors, with people discussing the situation on every corner. Excitement and apprehension crackled through the air in equal measure.

Word of troop movements had already reached the Valencourt house through the gossip of servants. Sarah wished word of Justin and the others' actions had also gotten there before her, but she knew that was impossible.

She wanted to weep when she saw her sister-in-law's expression change from welcome to fear as Addie studied her face.

"They've gone, haven't they?" she asked, and Sarah nodded. "Ad, too?"

"Yes, all three of them left this morning." Sarah drew a deep, steadying breath. "They were sorry to leave it to you, but if they aren't back by tonight or by tomorrow morning at the latest, you are to tell your father where they've gone."

Addie held perfectly still, afraid that if she moved, she would shatter. She had dreaded this for so long, she had thought that if it actually happened, she would be proof against the shock. Instead, she was more terrified than she had ever been in her life. She tried to tell herself that nothing was certain yet, that it was possible nothing would come of today's business, that the redcoats would return without firing a shot as they had from the failed raid on Salem. But she didn't believe it.

"I cannot stay here. I do not want to tell Papa anything until I must. And I cannot bear his satisfaction. He is encouraged that at last the government will gain control of the 'rascals and smugglers.'"

"We will go to my house," Sarah said. The quaver in Addie's voice and the pallor of her face were so contrary to her normal composure, they gave Sarah the strength to take charge. It was she who sought out Tullia and made their excuses, pretending nothing was out of the ordinary. "I am kidnapping Addie for the day. There are things in my house that need to be rearranged, and I want her opinion."

Sarah had laughed at Justin when he claimed that Tullia had known what he and his siblings were doing every minute since their births, but now, pinned under her intense regard, she believed it.

"You will take good care of her, I know, like you care for my Justin."

So few words, yet Sarah felt as if she'd been given the highest praise.

When she rejoined Addie and they left the house, Sarah said, "She didn't ask, but I'm sure Tullia knows where the men have gone."

"She does," Addie agreed, "and she will understand why they had to go even though she'll worry. I hope that if I have to tell Papa, he will be as wise."

"But you doubt it, don't you?"

"Yes. Consider how your father will judge Justin if he learns the truth and then think of how much angrier my father will be."

They went on, both hoping their fathers would never need know. The day seemed to stretch endlessly as they waited for news. And then by late afternoon, people along the shore could hear the thud of muskets in the distance, could even see the flashes from the firing pans and muzzles.

Addie and Sarah had alternated between huddling in the house, trying to talk about anything except what might be happening, and taking walks to collect the latest rumors. But once there were repeated reports of a battle, they climbed Copp's Hill and found others using the vantage point.

No one was quite sure what was happening. One man, peering through his spyglass, muttered, "It looks as if there are redcoats in Charlestown." But no one knew what that signified.

Addie shivered, endeavoring to ignore the fact that Copp's Hill was the site of an old burying ground.

As they walked back down the hill, they discussed the most likely explanation for the redcoats being in Charlestown.

"We know they crossed by boat toward Cambridge last night and marched over the Neck this morning, so why would they be in Charlestown now?" Sarah wondered.

They passed Christ Church, a reminder of Justin and Sarah's wedding and of happier times, and Addie kept thinking the unthinkable. "The only advantage the redcoats would have in Charlestown is protection from the guns of their fleet," she mused. "And the only reason they would need that would be if they were losing the battle. Otherwise, it would be easier for them to come back across the Neck."

They stopped in unison and stared at each other.

"Do you think it truly possible that we've won the day?" Sarah asked, and Addie wished Justin could hear his wife's unhesitating identification with the Patriots.

"I believe it's possible, and I will believe that Justin, Ad, and Silas are safe unless I hear otherwise," Addie said.

"Then I will have faith, too."

When they arrived back at Sarah's house, Addie took her leave. "I must go home, but if I can, I will wait until tomorrow to tell Papa."

"I also would rather wait to tell my parents, but I fear we may not have so much time." Sarah put her arms around Addie in a quick embrace. "This house belongs to Justin and to me. As long as I am here, there will be a place for you."

"Thank you." It was all Addie could manage without breaking down. She was chagrined to remember that she had once thought of Sarah as rather simple. Nothing could be further from the truth. And by her words, Sarah had made it clear that she understood everything about their current situation, including the fact that there was no way to know how the redcoats in Boston would deal with the families of Patriots, let alone how Loyalists would deal with members of their families who had chosen the other side.

Addie passed through the streets unmolested, but there were redcoats scurrying hither and yon, and they looked as confused as the civilians.

*

Any hope that there was yet time before Addie's father had to know the truth vanished the instant she arrived home. He was waiting for her in his library.

"I was ready to send a messenger for you. I had begun to doubt that you were with Sarah."

"And where else would I have been, Papa?" she asked cautiously.

"With your brothers and Silas, wherever they are. I have just returned from the shops. The three left this morning. No one knows where they went or when they will return. But you know, don't you, Ariadne?"

She could not remember the last time he had used her real name. She faced him across the desk, and the cold formality of his demeanor and voice chilled her to the bone. She met his eyes squarely, weighing her options. She could disclaim all knowledge at least until morning and perhaps beyond. She did not, after all, know for sure where the men had gone or what had happened. But suddenly it seemed to her that her father had as much right to the knowledge she did possess as she.

"You know redcoats left the town last night and this morning?" she asked.

He nodded but said nothing.

"No one except General Gage and his staff knew for a certainty where the soldiers were going, but the assumption was that they wanted to capture delegates to the Continental Congress as well as military stores. I think the militia turned out to stop them." She took a deep breath. "Justin, Ad, and Silas went to fight with the militia. They are pledged to the cause of justice, Papa. They are willing to risk their lives for it. They are willing to risk your love for it, and that must be hardest of all for them."

The silence stretched between them, a vast, unchartered space. The stern-faced Englishman staring at her bore no resemblance to the indulgent parent she knew. Addie thought nothing could be worse than this, but then her father's face changed again. He withered before her eyes, all his usual vitality seeping away to leave his face ravaged by grief and betrayal.

"How could they?" His voice was so low, Addie could barely make out the words.

She wanted desperately to explain so that he would understand. "They could do nothing else. You taught them to think clearly and to trust reason. For them, it is not reasonable to submit to tyranny. They can no longer tolerate being ill-treated by the government."

"They will be hanged for treason." Again it was such a small whisper of sound, Addie had to strain to hear.

He was not exaggerating. Under the Coercion Acts, local courts and local government had lost their teeth. People suspected of treasonous acts could be arrested and shipped to England for trial. Her brothers and Silas could be executed there. Her heart pounded so hard at the thought, she felt light-headed. And then the world steadied.

"Papa, they are not alone. I know you want to believe this is the work of just a small group of agitators. But that's not true. There are thousands who believe as Justin, Ad, and Silas do. And there are rumors that the redcoats are on the run."

"It is not possible!" Utter disbelief restored power to Marcus's voice.

"It is if enough men have made the same decision your sons and Silas made."

Her heart went out to him. He was torn by conflicting emotions. He could not believe that the British Army could be successfully challenged by the militia, but the lives of his sons and Silas depended on it.

"We will simply have to wait until a true account of the day is discovered," Addie pointed out, and then she asked, "Do you wish to know if I have chosen sides?"

Marcus bowed his head. "No. I do not need to hear you say it. I know where you stand. You would not defend your brothers so eloquently if you did not share their convictions."

Addie clasped her hands together to control their shaking. "Do you want me to leave your house? Sarah would take me in."

Marcus did not hesitate. "You are my daughter, whom I love. This is your home. And I doubt you plan to bear arms against the King. To entertain treasonous thoughts in one's mind is not the same as committing the act."

At that moment, Addie felt such pity for him, she dug her nails into her hands to transfer the pain so that her tears would not overflow. Marcus had always believed that nothing was stronger than the mind; than ideas and the beliefs men held. But now he was reduced to qualifying his convictions, to allow his daughter to remain under his roof and to determine what line beyond forgiveness his sons and Silas had crossed. And she realized that in all the questions he had not asked, in the very fact that he had gone in search of the young men, Marcus had suspected the truth, had probably suspected it for a long time.

"I should have insisted that Justin stay longer in England. I should have made sure that Ad attended school there, too. I should never have allowed him to go to that seditious college in New Jersey. I should have been firmer with Silas. I should have…" He seemed hardly aware of her as he enumerated to himself the ways he might have prevented the defections.

"Papa, please stop! You raised fine young men, and you raised them to think for themselves. You cannot condemn them or yourself for that!" But she saw by his face that he did. He didn't seem to notice when she left the room.

Needing comfort, she went to Tullia and was enfolded instantly in her arms. Tullia didn't ask questions, she just crooned and soothed as if Addie were a small child again. Then she said, "Won't do you any good to worry about them. They're together. They'll keep each other safe."

Tullia spoke with such conviction, Addie felt the burden on her heart lighten.

"Time will come when you'll have to move on," Tullia said, "but for now, you stay. Your papa, he needs you, and the mistress does, too. She hasn't told yet, but she's going to have another baby."

Addie's immediate reaction was joy. Marcus doted on baby Clement, and the prospect of another child would gratify him and might divert his attention somewhat from brooding over the action taken by his sons and Silas.

"I'll pretend to be surprised when Mary tells me," Addie assured Tullia, and then she asked, "Has anyone spoken to Quentin about what's happened?"

"I told him. Sometimes that boy gets neglected. No one means to leave him out of things, it's just that he lives so much inside his own self, it's easy to forget what happens to this family happens to him as well."

"How did he react?"

"Like it was no surprise to him, like he'd known something like this was bound to happen. Whatever he thinks about it inside… well, he'll tell it when he's ready."

Addie checked on Quentin before they gathered with their father and stepmother for a light supper. She meant to try to ease Quentin's anxiety, but he didn't share her fears; he was confident that his brothers and Silas were such good soldiers, no redcoats could possibly harm them.

Addie knew it was best that he felt that way, but his attitude emphasized what she was learning step by painful step. This was the province of males. Even the most logical of them seemed to discern an appealing symmetry in the chaos of war. Even Quentin, with his orderly approach to life, was attracted to it. She could see it in the light in his dark eyes. She shivered inwardly, remembering the battle orders he could coax from a fife. She wanted to demand his promise that he not get involved in the trouble, but she did not dare to mention the possibility, as if by so doing, she might spur him to action.

Supper was a torturous affair of long silences, each of the four trying to avoid any mention of the subject that was on all of their minds. Addie wished that little Peter and Jane had not already been fed and put to bed. The chatter of the children would have provided a welcome distraction.

Addie didn't think she could sleep at all that night, but exhaustion provided her with a few hours of oblivion. When morning came, all of Boston knew what had happened. More than half of the thirty-five hundred officers and men of the British force stationed in Boston had gone out on the Concord raid. They had been chosen because they were the best trained and the most experienced. The Patriots had soundly defeated them. There were reports that the British had sixty or seventy killed and upwards of two hundred wounded. Patriot losses were said to be much less. In exchange for not burning the town during their retreat, the British had been allowed to shelter in Charlestown, and the selectmen of the town promised to help in the evacuation. The soldiers clustered on the sloping ground of Bunker Hill. They were without provisions, and many were so fatigued as to fall asleep the moment they lay down. Some of the wounded died there, having suffered the rough journey from Lexington. Boats from British ships came across to get the wounded off first and then the rest of Percy's force.

The Loyalists in Boston were shocked, while those who supported the Patriots could not rejoice too openly. They were still under British rule, and many were fearful about what punishment might be visited on them.

Addie's pity for her father increased. Marcus had aged further overnight. He found it nearly impossible to believe the redcoats had been defeated, and yet, despite his growing fury at what his sons and Silas had done, the report of low casualties among the militia was good news to him. He did not want to hear that Justin or Ad or Silas had been killed.

It was news Addie also dreaded, and she fretted about how word would be gotten into Boston if it were true. Needing to be away from her father's pain and from the accusation she saw in his eyes when he looked at her, she spent much of the day with Sarah.

"If something had happened to any of them, someone would tell us," Sarah insisted.

They both needed to believe it, despite not knowing how it would be accomplished.

Sarah admitted she had an advantage in having her own household. "I think my mother is more frightened and confused than anything else, but my father is so angry! I could not bear to be in his presence all day long."

Addie nodded. "It is the same for me with Papa. But my situation is different. I still have Quentin at home, and Mary and her children and Tullia. Somehow I feel as if I need to be there for all of them, at least for now, until we see what is going to happen next. I am grateful, though, that I can come here."

In the ensuing days, she had growing reason for that gratitude. Life in Boston changed, the city becoming more and more a British military post as many civilians abandoned the city. General Gage made no effort to stop the exodus, despite his strong suspicion that most of those leaving were in sympathy with the Rebels, as they were now frequently labeled, as if in recognition that they were proving too dangerous to be dismissed as mere provincials. However, Gage did forbid the departing to take any possessions with them, thus any who did join the Rebels would do so with little more than the clothes on their backs.

"Damned Rebels," Marcus fumed, "they ought to be confined to the city to ensure the safety of those of us who are loyal to the government."

He seemed to go out of his way to disparage the Rebels in Addie's presence, as if he could thereby persuade her that her loyalty was misplaced. She heard the pain and fear under the anger. He did not mention her brothers or Silas, but she was sure he thought about them constantly. And there was good reason for any Loyalist to fear the future. Far from disappearing after the battles at Lexington and Concord, the provincial force continued to grow, the men gathering in Cambridge and the surrounding countryside. For the time being, the British were prisoners in besieged Boston.

At first, Marcus hadn't the slightest desire to leave the city. He wanted the protection of the British Army, and he clung to the idea that soon the Rebels would be dispersed outside of Boston, and the army would regain control of the countryside. However, less than two weeks after the battles, Mary could no longer conceal her pregnancy. She had wanted to wait before she added to her husband's worries, and she didn't know that Tullia's sharp eyes had already noted her condition. But suddenly Mary was too violently ill for most of the day to keep the secret.

Because she had not been sick when she carried Clement, Marcus's first reaction was terror that Mary was suffering from some lethal fever.

"I assure you, it is your child in my womb, not a fever that so unsettles me," she told him.

Marcus felt a mixture of joy, pride, and concern. It was one thing to stand fast in Boston when his family was healthy, but it was quite another when his wife was with child and ill, particularly when she had

had so little trouble during her previous pregnancies. He considered the matter for several days, and he arrived at his conclusion by the same logical process he used to make all important decisions.

Calmly, he announced his plan to Mary late one afternoon when her queasiness was at its lowest ebb. "With the boys gone, and things being what they are, I will have to attend closely to business here, but I think you and the children ought to go to the farm. The atmosphere will be less strained for you and better for our babe. When the present troubles are past, you can return here or I will join you at the farm."

He expected no disagreement, so it took him a moment to understand that Mary was shaking her head in negation, and then he saw tears begin to trickle down her cheeks.

"Marcus, one of the reasons I married you was that you are a rational man, a man of great intelligence. But of late, you have abandoned all sense. We cannot leave Boston, not now."

"It is not just those with rebellious beliefs who have left the city, Loyalists have gone, too," he protested.

"It is not the same for them," Mary said quietly. "They have not been as outspoken against the Patriots as you have been. They had not dined with General Gage nor openly urged him to crush the rebellion. They have not entertained scores of redcoats in their homes. Husband, you have made yourself an enemy to the Patriots, and they know who you are. I am your wife. Not even your sons and Silas could protect us from everyone who would punish us. Here we are safe, at least for the present; we would not be safe on the farm."

He wanted to deny the truth of what she said, but he remembered how government officials had been harried during the Stamp Act crisis and during the furor over the Tea Act. Houses had been sacked and their owners abused in many cities and towns. And now the situation was much worse. Now there was an army of villains waiting outside of Boston.

His mind fixed on the words Mary had used. "You call them Patriots. Are you on their side, too?"

A great wave of tenderness washed over Mary, tenderness for Marcus and for their unborn child. "I am on your side, always. That will never change. But I beg you to understand. I am American-born. I am not English in my heart as you are. My people came to this country more than a hundred years go. I don't agree with all of the Patriots' methods, but I agree with their belief that the government cannot continue to treat us as if we were inferior."

Marcus had never been surer of Mary's love for him, and he had never felt so isolated. He had lived in this country for thirty-five years, more than half of his life, and it seemed the country was not his at all. He had refused to believe that disaffected colonists could present any real threat. Now he saw through his wife's eyes that his stubborn insistence on proclaiming himself a loyal Englishman could endanger his family. The best he could hope was that Gage's troops would overcome resistance and crush the rebellion. Yet, if that occurred, two of his sons and Silas might well forfeit their lives.

He straightened his shoulders. He had not changed. His loyalty was steadfast and would continue so. It was those around him who had changed. They would have to live with and perhaps risk all for their choice. But there was one thing he could do for Mary.

"If you wish to leave Boston, and I do think it best, I could make it known that you and I have had a falling out, that my political beliefs are not yours. I could—"

She put up her hand to stay his words. "Do not make me more of a Patriot than I am. I mean what I say. No matter what I think of this business, my first loyalty is to you. The children and I will stay with you, whatever comes."

"You know that soldiers will still come to visit? I can scarcely ban them from the house now."

"I know. They have come since the day of battle, and I have not turned them away. Most of them are fine men who believe in their duty. In truth, I have come to feel sorry for them. They are so very far from home."

He was humbled by her generosity of spirit. "I will keep you and our children safe, I swear it," he said.

Mary gazed back at him with serene trust, allowing none of her doubts to show.

Like Mary, Addie accepted the complications of the divided loyalties of the house. She had little choice, but beyond that, she, no less than her stepmother, felt a stir of pity for the redcoats who visited. Many of them, including Captain Byrne, had taken part in the raid on Concord, and that action had shocked many out of their complacency.

Captain Byrne had a purple red mark on his cheek, legacy of a musket ball that had seared his skin but could easily have killed him. He knew how lucky he had been, and he was forthright about how the experience had changed his ideas.

"The older soldiers, the men who fought with the militia against the French and Indians, they have little good to say about their former allies. But I saw how the militia fought. They've learned something from the savages. They shot from cover, and they kept on and on. There were more and more of them by the hour. It seemed they came from every direction. And they are still gathering. I do not think the government understands the gravity of the situation."

"Well, I am relieved that the man who shot you was not quite accurate in his aim." Addie meant the words even as she rejoiced inwardly at his assessment of the Patriots' army. She was growing accustomed to this duality. Civil war seemed to have its own odd rules.

She suspected most of their military visitors knew that Justin, Ad, and Silas were gone. They might not have missed them from the house, as the young men had seldom been there with the redcoats, but the officers were used to seeing them in the shops. Now Marcus was spending more time in those establishments than he had in years, and Quentin was usually with him. And yet, none of the soldiers questioned Addie or anyone else in the family regarding the whereabouts of her brothers or Silas. Their names were not mentioned. Even Captain Byrne, who had seen how much she cared for Silas, said not a word to Addie about him.

It was surely easier this way, but it also gave Addie the eerie sense that her brothers and Silas had been judged guilty of such wickedness that so little as uttering their names might befoul the speaker.

"More than once I have had the impulse to announce, politely, you understand, that my brothers and Silas are brave, honorable men," she told Sarah.

"Pray do not give in to that impulse!" Sarah made a face. "I don't know how you can bear to treat the redcoats so civilly, but I admire you for it. If we ever leave, you will have interesting information to give to our side."

"I think I would make a most unlikely spy," Addie said, and she asked, "Do you think about it often, leaving the city?"

"Constantly. If Justin sends word for me to join him, I'll go. But I don't think he will. By all accounts, the Patriot camps are crowded, dirty, and have little place for families. And I do worry about my parents. I wish I were not their only child. They have ever spoiled and indulged me, but now I feel I am responsible for them. Under my father's anger, there is more fear every day. Part of me is relieved that Justin has not sent for me because I have not had to make the choice between him and my parents."

They continued to allow no doubt that the men were safe, and their faith was rewarded when a young man, scarcely more than a boy, bumped into Addie one day as she approached Sarah's house. With a mumbled apology, the lad was gone, and it took Addie a moment to realize he had pressed something into her hand.

She made no attempt to examine it and no mention of it until she and Sarah were alone, and then she whispered so no servant could overhear as she carefully unfolded what turned out to be a tight wad of paper. "This was passed to me outside, and maybe... oh, yes!" Her eyes filled with tears as she read the crabbed script. "Look! They are alive, all three of them!"

The piece of paper hadn't been large to begin with, and the tight folding had made myriad creases that made the script even harder to read, but Addie and Sarah deciphered the words.

Justin had written: "My darling wife, we are safe and well. Camp conditions are unpleasant, but our cause is just. Have patience, we will be together again."

Ad's message was for his twin: "Do not worry about us. Take care of Papa. I miss all of you."

They had each used only their first initial and had addressed the two women in the same way, but there was no doubt that the last message was from Silas to Addie.

She read the words once and then again, but they remained the same: "I miss you. I love you. Stay safe and well that we may wed as soon as possible."

Only as she understood the missive did Addie realize how little she had expected—to know that Silas and her brothers were safe, that was all. That Silas would send an avowal of his love had never occurred to her. The words blurred.

Wiping at her own tears, Sarah managed a smile. "Just look at us! The very news we've been awaiting, and we weep for it. But I must say, shy Silas seems to have grown bold."

"He has, hasn't he? He must have great hope for the Patriot cause." Addie hardly recognized the breathy voice as her own, and she watched in dazed fascination as Sarah took her sewing scissors and carefully cut off Justin's message, leaving the other two for Addie.

They wished they knew who the boy was who had carried the letter; they wished there were a way to send word in reply, but nothing was as important as knowing that the men were alive.

Addie's joy in Silas's message so filled her that at first she could see no drawbacks, and then she thought a little more clearly. "I cannot tell Papa. I want to, but I can't. He would want to know how I learned of their safety. I don't dare tell him that a messenger found me."

"You don't dare look as happy as you did a moment ago, either, unless you want to betray yourself," Sarah cautioned.

"I'm normally quite happy," Addie protested.

"Not like that, you're not. Only Silas makes you look like that. I shall have to be careful, too, lest my parents suspect I have heard from Justin. But my case is not so serious. I do not have so much contact with redcoats. Pray remember, you are welcome to stay here with me."

It was tempting. If she lived with Sarah, she would not have to be so guarded in everything she did and said as she was in her father's house. But immediately she recalled the ties of duty and affection that bound her there; they were no less because she had heard from Silas.

"My answer must still be no," she told the other woman with regret.

She found she had to keep Sarah's warning in mind because the image of Silas kept sweeping over her, making it hard not to laugh aloud for the joy of the words he had sent to her.

And despite her care, Quentin, who so seldom seemed to notice those around him, told her, "You look different. You look happier than I can ever remember."

She wanted to tell him the truth, show him the words from Ad and Silas, but she didn't. It was hard enough for her not to tell their father; she wasn't sure Quentin could resist the temptation, particularly because he worked with Marcus so much of the time now.

"I am happy for a lot of reasons. It's spring. Clement is growing by the day and will soon have a new brother or sister, and you're doing so well working with Papa."

Quentin didn't appear completely convinced, but he was distracted by her mention of work. "Papa is pretending everything is as it was, but that isn't true. I know it hurts him that the *Chronicle* is no longer being published. There's no need for it in this military encampment with another man favored as Royal printer, despite Papa's loyalty. And though we still have a good inventory in the shops, we have it because Papa paid no attention to the refusal of British goods. But the only way he can obtain more stock is through the British, from British ships. Perhaps such goods will continue to come in for a while longer, but the Patriots are preventing anything from the countryside getting into Boston. When the weather grows cold again, how will the soldiers here feed themselves? How will the citizens get food? Everything will have to come in by ship, and I doubt there will be room for the newest novels or music or fine paper. Papa won't be destitute. He has good credit with his bankers in London, his properties here are valuable, and there is a respectable fortune in silver at the house. But as long as this war, or whatever one calls it, goes on, Papa's enterprises will suffer."

"There is always Darius in New York."

"Yes, but Darius has done the same as Papa. He has ignored the ban on British goods and has been open in his Tory sympathies, much to Papa's pride. If the whole country is roused to rebellion, he, too, will be safe only under British guns and prosperous only to the extent they allow."

It was a revelation to Addie to listen to Quentin. He had always been the baby among Lily's children, but no longer. His assessments made sense. And while he might be working with their father, he didn't share his politics. The way he spoke of "the British" made it clear that he now considered himself separate from them.

It did not occur to her until it was too late that Quentin had been keeping secrets of his own. Two weeks after their conversation, he was gone. He had taken little with him when he slipped out of the town, but his artist's case and his fife were missing.

His note to Addie was short: "I am sorry I couldn't face you. I didn't want you to try to stop me. I must go. Do not worry about me. I will find our brothers and Silas."

He had left a note for Marcus, too, and Addie was grateful for that, but it didn't make it any easier to witness their father's grief. She thought it would have been more bearable had Marcus ranted, but instead he accepted the news silently and looked older and grayer. The Marcus of the past would have made some attempt to go after Quentin or to have him brought back for his own safety, but now he understood that events and his sons had moved beyond his control.

His attitude made Addie feel even more protective of him than before. Mary was doing her best to offer comfort, but she continued to be plagued by sickness that lasted most of the day, and her condition added to Marcus's worries.

Addie didn't ask her father's permission; she simply started accompanying him to work. She wrote a fair hand and could easily do accounts, and in the Boston created by the siege, few took exception to her working with her father. She had less time to spend with Sarah, but Sarah understood and braved more contact with redcoats in order to come by the bookstore to lend quiet support to Addie.

Addie tried to help in the printing office as well, for even without the newspaper, there were still jobs to do there. But though she was fairly adept at setting type, the actual operation of the press was better left to others. Every day was a reminder of the skills her brothers and Silas had taken with them, and though Marcus hired more staff, the operation of both the bookstore and the printing office was far less efficient than before.

Addie also worried about Tullia. She had had so much to do with raising Lily's children, it was as if they were her own, and yet she had no say in their futures. Addie knew how concerned she was about her "boys," but Tullia was too accustomed to taking care of others to accept solace for herself. Instead, she turned her energies to planning a larger vegetable garden than usual, though the gardens around the house had long yielded bountiful harvests.

"There is little in the markets now and will be less and less," she said. "People in this house won't go hungry, if I can help it."

Tullia wasn't the only one in town making such changes. Many of the remaining civilians who had land around their houses were cultivating the earth for food rather than ornamentation. And soldiers, many quartered on the Common now that the weather was warmer, were also planting plots of vegetables.

It was clear the British were anticipating an attack from the massed Rebels, and yet those in command continued to speak as if the situation would somehow right itself.

Toward the end of May, three generals, Sir William Howe, Sir Henry Clinton, and "Gentleman Johnny" Burgoyne, joined Gage in Boston. Gage was to remain as governor of the province, but General Howe, with Clinton and Burgoyne serving under him, assumed command of the British troops.

Though Burgoyne had no connections to the colonies, Addie thought that Howe and Clinton's past histories must cause them some distress in the current situation. Howe and his two older brothers had fought in the French and Indian War, and the siblings had been admired by the colonists. Clinton was the son of Admiral George Clinton and had spent his youth in New York while his father had been governor there. Both Howe and Clinton had many friends in America, and undoubtedly some of those friends counted themselves as Patriots.

Clinton was a small, fair, slack-muscled man whose dour and somewhat clerkish demeanor belied the fact that he was a professional soldier. He was quite colorless compared to Howe and Burgoyne. Howe was tall and dark, with a big nose, black eyes, and obvious signs of being well fed. He exuded a congeniality that was hard to resist. But Burgoyne was far more flamboyant and within days of his arrival, his history was the favorite topic of gossip.

More than thirty years before, General Burgoyne and the Lady Charlotte, daughter of the Earl of Derby, had eloped. Within a few years, financial pressures had forced Burgoyne to sell his commission in the army, and the young couple had gone to live in France for a time. Burgoyne was intelligent and witty, and by all accounts he had enjoyed his exposure to French culture, but eventually his father-in-law's attitude softened, and the earl helped Burgoyne get another commission in the army. He had acquitted himself well during the Seven Years War, the conflict that had engulfed most of Europe from 1756 to 1763, while the French and Indian War raged in the colonies. Once back in London after the war, Burgoyne won a seat in Parliament and took his place among the fashionable people of the city, being accepted by the best clubs and earning a reputation as an avid gambler. But he also became known as an amateur playwright and an actor of some promise.

Addie first met him when he came to the bookstore. He was a large, handsome man in his early fifties, and though an experienced soldier, he handled books as if they were fragile, living things, his face lighting with pleasure when he recognized favorite titles. He treated her and her father with grave courtesy, and it was obvious that Marcus had been identified to him as a staunch Loyalist. When Marcus invited him to the house, General Burgoyne accepted with alacrity.

When he visited, he praised Marcus's private library, and the two men fell to discussing several works, the talk continuing as they rejoined other guests, mainly junior officers, and Addie. Addie listened to the two men, and she couldn't help but admire the skillful way Burgoyne drew her father out, leading him through a description of recent events in and around Boston and asking finally, "How far do you judge your countrymen are willing to go to achieve their ends?"

Addie watched her father's face as he considered his answer, and she knew the instant he decided to mention her brothers. He looked as much relieved as resigned.

"General, I can't speak for all of my countrymen, not for the Loyalists or the Rebels, but I can tell you that three of my sons have left me to stand against His Majesty's forces. Two of them and another young man, who seemed like a son to me, left the day of the battles at Lexington and Concord, and I do not know if they survived. My son Quentin quit this house just recently. This is only his fifteenth year. I did not want to believe it before, but if there are many like my sons, then…" His voice trailed off, and he shrugged.

"Then we can only hope that the conflict is quickly brought to a peaceful resolve," Burgoyne said, as if finishing Marcus's sentence.

Addie wanted to say that it would take a revolution in Parliament for that to happen, but she held her tongue, and she was touched when General Burgoyne said to her, "You must miss your brothers a great deal, Mistress Valencourt."

"Indeed, I do, sir," she agreed and left it at that. She did not doubt the genuineness of the general's sympathy. He was called "Gentleman Johnny" not for his urbane ways, but because he believed in treating the men under his command well and deplored the harsh punishments meted out in the military.

In the early days of June, another visitor appeared to pay his respects. There could be no doubt any more that the Scotsman, John Traverne, was in the colonies at the government's behest, else he would not have been in the besieged port where only Loyalists seeking shelter from the Patriot-held countryside and people on official missions were allowed in.

Addie puzzled over why the watchfulness of his dark gaze so discomfited her. There was no secret now about where her brothers and Silas had gone, so it wasn't as if she had to worry about betraying them. She didn't want to concern herself with Mr. Traverne at all, but something had changed in him since the last time she'd seen him. It made her cross that she'd noticed enough about him to see the change, but she was also curious. He seemed melancholy, and it was hard to imagine that the political situation in the colonies could cause that reaction in him. But whenever Addie glanced at him, she saw the shadows in his eyes, the lines graven deeper in his rather harsh face, making him look older.

Finally, she approached him as if pulled by a magnet.

"You do not look well, sir. Tullia, our housekeeper, is skilled with herbs and potions. Would you like to consult with her?" As she spoke, she remembered asking Silas the same thing not so long ago.

John Traverne was physically tired and soul weary, and the last thing he had expected was attention from the elusive Mistress Valencourt. He was so surprised, he told the truth. "I thank you for your offer, but it is no ailment your woman can cure. I have had sad news from home; it has been long months finding me. It makes me wish I had never left Scotland."

She didn't say the words to ask for more information, but her golden eyes seemed to pull him in.

"My wife Jeane was expecting our first child when I sailed. She and the babe died."

Addie had a mad impulse to put her arms around the big man to comfort him, but the best she could do was to tender her sympathy. "I am so sorry. I know it is not much to offer, but pray feel welcome here. It is not, I realize, the same as your own family, but at least you will have company."

"Thank you," he said again, "but this will be my last visit here. I am returning home. I came today to bid farewell, to express my gratitude for your previous hospitality, and to ask if you have any special messages you wish me to carry to your sister."

Marcus did have word to send to Callista, but Addie did not. It was not that she harbored any animosity toward her half-sister; it was just that with the twelve-year age difference between them, they hardly knew each other. Callista's life in England, complete with husband, children, a country estate, and other properties, had no bearing on Addie's life in Boston.

With a strange feeling of regret, Addie wished Mr. Traverne Godspeed. Despite his family tragedy and obligations, she was sure he would report to the government in England before he went home to Scotland. He had made her uneasy from the first, and until this day, they had not exchanged any personal words. Yet the glimpse she had had of his sorrow intrigued her; it was such a contrast to the implacable strength she had sensed in him before. There was an interesting story in this man, a story she would never know in its entirety.

"Care well for yourself, Mistress Valencourt. These are dangerous times." With those brief words, he was gone.

Addie shivered, her mood shifting until she felt only relief that John Traverne was leaving. It would be better for her brothers and Silas if he never returned to America. If he were as good a soldier as she suspected, she would not like to know he was fighting against the Patriots.

Since the battles of April 19, there had been little fighting except for skirmishes when the British had tried to gather fodder for their livestock from islands in the harbor. Addie and Sarah began to hope that perhaps the war would go no further and would be settled without more bloodshed. And that would mean that men like John Traverne would not be needed by either side.

The hope was short-lived. Rumor spread like fire that with the change of command, the British had also acquired a plan to attack Rebel headquarters in Cambridge.

The Patriots struck first. Under cover of darkness on June 16, militia moved onto the Charlestown peninsula and, digging furiously all night, they fortified a position on Breed's Hill. The little town of Charlestown was almost deserted and had been since shortly after the battles, the inhabitants having realized how vulnerable they were to redcoats and to shots from British ships.

At six o'clock the next morning, the new fortifications and the tiny figures of dark-clothed militia still digging were spotted from the ship *Lively*. A shot was fired from the ship to alert the British forces on other ships and on shore. Boston was soon astir as redcoats scrambled out of their beds in all quarters of the town and civilians roused as well.

It was Saturday, and Addie had planned to go to work with her father as usual, but she quickly changed course. "I am going to spend the day with Sarah," she told him.

He nodded, mumbling, "I don't suppose there is any cause to open the shops today, anyway." He did not say the words, but his grave expression betrayed the fact that he was thinking of his sons and Silas, not of business.

On her way across town, Addie saw scores of redcoats hurrying to join their companies. Some were bidding farewell to wives or sweethearts, and she looked away.

Addie had grown to depend on Sarah's strength, but it wasn't in evidence today. Sarah fell into her arms, trembling.

"Oh, thank God you have come! I couldn't go to my parents. I could not bear it if they cheer the redcoats on."

Addie held her close and patted her back until the trembling eased.

"I need to keep watch," Sarah said. "Justin might be there."

"If he is, so will the others be," Addie said.

They climbed Copp's Hill as they had on the day the British had retreated to Charlestown, but this time it was the Patriots who seemed vulnerable.

Addie frowned, staring into the distance at the figures that looked like ants. "There must be some good reason, but I can't imagine it. Why would they try to secure a position that is vulnerable to British guns?"

Sarah was as anxious to understand as Addie, but she couldn't. "Mayhap Justin and the others aren't there. It isn't the whole army, after all," was the best she could offer.

They were not the only ones who had turned out to see what would happen. Any high point in Boston or in the surrounding countryside with a view of the Charlestown area was soon clustered with watchers.

Addie felt the pounding in her heart when British cannon from the Copp's Hill battery opened fire on Charlestown, and she and Sarah stared in horror as the town caught fire. Wooden church steeples became spires of flame reaching high into the sky, and burning buildings collapsed on each other. They could hear the roar of the firestorm across the water.

They watched the rows of barges taking the redcoats across, so many soldiers that the barges had to make two trips. It was such a colorful sight, it was as if a magnificent pageant were being staged for the delight of spectators. Except that some of these players would surely die before the sun set.

British troop movements were not the only ones; additional Patriot forces were spotted crossing Charlestown Neck, daring the reach of the guns on British ships.

Addie and Sarah weren't aware of thirst or hunger or any other physical discomfort as they watched the day and the action unfold. They were scarcely aware of the press of other observers or of the presence of generals Clinton and Burgoyne and their aides close by at the battery.

The first clash came when the Welsh Fusiliers, with other companies behind them, began to advance along the narrow beach. If they could follow that route far enough they could attack the rear of Breed's Hill. But Patriots sheltered behind the rocks waited until their targets were within range, and then they opened fire. The fusiliers toppled like toy soldiers swept by a giant hand.

Grenadiers marching along above the beach could not see what was happening below, but they met their match in the militia waiting for them behind fences, waiting until they could fire to greatest effect.

The British artillery was struggling to get their guns into place, having to drag heavy equipment out of marshy ground, so their troops were not getting the support they expected.

Addie wanted to look away from the slaughter but could not. Time seemed to move swiftly and slowly at once. Even the stray musket shots that made it as far as Copp's Hill did not distract her from the battle. Beside her, Sarah was equally transfixed.

The Patriots fell back to Breed's Hill in good order after inflicting heavy casualties on the British. Then the first wave of redcoats assaulted the hill and fell in great numbers as the Patriots again held fire until their enemies were nearly upon them. The British attack was broken, but they rallied and came at the hill again, to be rebuffed once more.

General Howe had been directing the action at the scene for some time, and Clinton had left Copp's Hill and crossed to join the fray after seeing the losses being inflicted on the British.

Sarah's hand crept into Addie's, and Addie held it tightly.

"No one should have to die so, not even redcoats," Sarah whispered.

Addie cringed inside, dreading that some of the fallen enemy would prove to be soldiers who had visited the Valencourt house.

The redcoats marched forward and upward in a third charge.

"God help us," Addie breathed as she watched, for this time it was different. The British kept going, and the Patriots could be seen falling back. Now the vulnerability of the position on Breed's Hill, indeed on the Charlestown peninsula, was revealed, for the narrow, exposed isthmus offered little encouragement to reinforcements with the British guns coming into play and could prove treacherous for retreat.

Addie and Sarah continued to watch, scarcely drawing breath, until finally it dawned on them that though the British might claim victory for the day, it was at such cost, as there appeared to be little pursuit of the retreating Patriots, who were withdrawing without panic.

After the carnage they had witnessed, the women felt numb. And the people around them, surely overwhelmingly Loyalist in sympathy, were equally stunned.

"Christ's blood! If we win very many more such victories, all will be lost," a man swore.

It was only then that Addie realized that the voice was easy to hear, that the enormous din of the day, the roar of cannon, the crack of musketry, the high pitch of fifes, and the low pound of drums had ceased.

Smoke from the burning of Charlestown and from the battle hung in the air. It reminded Addie of a great funeral pyre, and she imagined she could smell death across the water.

Chapter 9

It took two days to ferry all the British wounded and dead back to Boston, but overnight, the city turned into a charnel house. The British had committed more than two thousand of their troops to the battle, and their casualties were said to be nearly fifty percent with more than two hundred killed and more than eight hundred wounded. And the loss among the officer corps was very high, including all of General Howe's aides, who had been hit as they kept their posts beside him.

When the wounded started to arrive in the city, Loyalists sent every conveyance they had, from coaches to handbarrows, to the waterside to assist in transporting them. All the physicians, surgeons, apothecaries, and anyone else with medical knowledge presented themselves to minister to the injured.

Marcus offered all the help he could, including taking in several wounded officers, and Addie was in complete agreement with him. She could not witness suffering without trying to ease it, and she hoped if her brothers or Silas were wounded, someone would aid them, without consideration of which side they were on. She was thankful that Tullia was of like mind, for she knew more about healing than most physicians, and her gentle methods were far less likely to add to suffering.

But Addie's determinedly calm acceptance of the situation was badly shaken when she discovered that one of their patients was Captain Byrne. A fellow officer who had also visited with the Valencourts had arranged for the captain to be brought to them.

Byrne had been hit in the right side of his chest and in his right thigh. He had lost so much blood before his wounds had been bound he was unconscious when he was brought to the house. Addie would have thought him dead had she not seen the slight rise and fall of his chest.

Addie turned so pale at the sight of him, Tullia said, "You don't have to help with this one."

Those words stiffened Addie's spine, and she thought of what a tolerant friend the captain had proved to be. He knew how she felt about Silas, and though they had never discussed it, he surely knew Silas had gone to fight with the Patriots. Yet he had never treated her with anything except courtesy.

"I do have to help him," she told Tullia.

Tullia's rules for healing were simple—to keep the patient clean, quiet, neither too warm nor too cold, and to use medications sparingly. She did not see any sense in bleeding, purging, blistering, and otherwise abusing a person who was already ill.

Mary was still too queasy with her pregnancy to be of much use, and Tullia was not prudish about allowing Addie to aid her. As far as Tullia was concerned, the sick, no matter what age, were like needy children.

Captain Byrne was not so at ease. For the first couple of days he drifted in and out of consciousness with no awareness of where he was. And then he opened his eyes and recognized Ariadne Valencourt. She was bathing his face and neck and had gotten to his arms before he gathered the strength to whisper, "No."

Addie understood. Continuing to cool his hot skin, she explained about the wounded being cared for all over Boston. "You belong here, Captain. You must rest and let us help you."

He was in too much pain, too exhausted, and her ministrations felt too good for him to protest further. He closed his eyes again.

The next time he opened them, it was to find Tullia checking his bandages with gentle hands, and the time after that it was Addie again, urging him to drink broth from the cup she held to his mouth. He decided to cease being embarrassed by the good fortune of being in the hands of caring women rather than those of some rough barber surgeon.

In addition to Captain Byrne, four other wounded redcoats had been brought to the Valencourt home, so Addie, Tullia, and the housemaids had their hands full. To Addie's surprise, Sarah came to help and stayed for long hours.

"After seeing them fall like that, well, it doesn't matter what color their coats are," she explained.

They had had no word from their men after the battle, but Patriot casualties had been many fewer than those of the British, so they continued to trust that no hurt had come to their own. But the Patriots had suffered a grievous loss in the death of Dr. Joseph Warren. He had been so bright and personable, there were many Loyalists who mourned him, despite his fierce devotion to the Rebels.

On the British side, with all the losses, the man most mourned was Major Pitcairn. He was the one who had been in command of the advance guard at Lexington. His contempt for provincials had proven mortally ill-founded. He had been popular among the British troops and with Loyalists, and his death during the last charge at Breed's Hill was given added poignancy because he had died in the arms of his son, an ensign in the marines. Ensign Pitcairn had helped to carry his father's body to a boat.

The action was being called the "Battle of Bunker Hill" despite the fact that Breed's Hill had been the site. But rumor had it that the Patriots had been in some disagreement over which hill to fortify and had even been confused about which hill was which on the night they had dug in. And the British were equally confused and had switched the names of the hills on their charts. Addie didn't care what they called the battle or which hill had been involved. She wished the battle had never happened, anywhere. And even as she wished it, she understood that this was only the beginning. She knew her brothers and Silas would never back down.

Meanwhile, there were reports that the Second Continental Congress was voting to support Massachusetts in its struggle against the government. Though it was all her brothers and Silas hoped for, Addie could scarcely imagine how it would work. She thought of her relatives in Virginia, Patriots, but so different from the people in New England. All the talk, all the discussions and promises would have to be put to some practical use. It was that practicality that worried her. The delegates from the various colonies had managed to work together last year, but these men were the best educated, most able of their colonies. To fight a war, the cooperation would have to be on a much broader scale. It was hard to picture New Englanders fighting beside men from New York or Pennsylvania or the Southern colonies. Most colonists knew only their region and way of life and distrusted anyone who was different; only a small percentage had traveled enough to have a wider view. It was this circumstance that had made Lily's marriage to Marcus so unusual. Yet, the marriage had pleased both of them until Lily died. Perhaps if the colonists could come together two by two, they might be able to forge some sort of union against the British, Addie thought wryly.

It was frustrating to be cut off from news of what was happening outside of Boston. There were rumors, and there were sanctioned reports, but they were slanted to give the government's version.

Captain Byrne did not share the government's optimism regarding suppressing the rebelliousness of the colonies. "The battle did not end because we won. It ended because the Rebels ran out of ammunition," he told Addie. He was still very weak and tired easily, but he seemed to need to talk about the battle with no pretense. "I want to understand. They aren't professional soldiers, but they fought well. I want to understand what means so much to them that they would risk their lives so."

Addie tried to explain, and in the effort she came to understand better than ever before how far from England she, her brothers, Silas, and thousands of others had drifted.

"The rights you speak of, most Englishmen don't enjoy them either," the captain protested. "The great majority of the country lives in poverty and has little voice in the government."

"I think you argue better for the Patriots' cause than I," she told him, and he smiled ruefully at being caught so neatly in his own trap. But then he sobered. "The government will not back down, not now. And though there may be many Rebels in this colony, there are also many who are loyal to the King and Parliament, men like your father. And I have heard there are far more Loyalists in the Middle and Southern colonies than in this region. Surely they, with His Majesty's forces, will be enough to subdue the rebellion."

"Are you telling me that it will be so or asking me?"

He moved restlessly, then quieted with a grimace as his wounds protested. "I think I am trying to convince myself," he admitted.

"And I think you should rest now. Neither of us can change anything today." She touched his face, feeling that he still had a fever, though not as high as it had been.

He closed his eyes and was instantly asleep. A chill moved over her skin. When his blue eyes were alight with interest, he looked as if he were getting stronger, but in sleep he appeared very frail.

"I believe Captain Byrne is recovering nicely, don't you?" Addie said to Tullia, and she heard the same mixture of assertiveness and doubt that she had pointed out to the captain.

"The bullets are out, the wounds are as clean as we can make them, and the captain was a fit man before he was shot. That is all to the good." Tullia studied Addie's face as she spoke. "But he lost much blood before he was brought to us, he has not had a day without fever, the flesh is falling away from his bones, and he is weak. We can hope, and we can care well for him. But, child, don't set your heart too much on him." Not even the softness of Tullia's voice blunted the sharp impact of her words.

Addie turned away, not wanting Tullia to see too much, knowing she would anyway. She was not in love with Captain Byrne. She was in love with Silas. However, though she and the captain were political enemies, she liked him as a human being, and she felt as if their odd friendship was a symbol, albeit a small one, that the differences between England and her colonies might not be irreconcilable. She was determined that the captain would recover, but she could not refuse when he asked her to write a letter for him.

It was a straightforward message to his family, telling them what had happened to him, telling them that he loved them, and had done his best for King and country.

Addie's quill faltered halfway through. "But this, this…"

"This is just in case," he said firmly. "If I die, my commanding officer will undoubtedly write to them, too, but I would feel better knowing that they had heard directly from me." His eyes held hers. "Please."

"As you wish, but I will not need to send this." She kept writing, blushing at the kind tribute to the care he had received from the Valencourts, a tribute he insisted be part of the letter.

"I want them to know I was treated with great kindness here, and that I was not alone."

She blinked away tears, not wanting them to fall and smudge the script, and she set down every word as he wanted it.

A little more than two weeks after the battle, rumors from Philadelphia were confirmed. The Second Continental Congress had not only voted to support Massachusetts in its struggle against British oppression, it had put teeth in the measure by designating the forces surrounding Boston as part of the Continental Army and by choosing George Washington as Commander in Chief.

Captain Byrne seemed a little stronger by the day, and when he heard from fellow officers about the arrival of Washington at Rebel headquarters in Cambridge, he was eager to question Addie.

"Do you know this Mr. Washington?" he asked, though he thought it unlikely.

She saw his surprise when she answered, "I do. And it is 'General'"—she relished the sound of Washington's new rank—"unless it is also 'Mr.' Clinton, 'Mr.' Burgoyne, and 'Mr.' Howe." She knew that he, like other redcoats, would not acknowledge the rank of the Rebel military.

He grinned at her. "We will have to keep our separate addresses. But pray, tell me of him."

"He is a good, steady man. He has military experience. He served in the French and Indian War. He is a Virginia planter and innovative in his farming methods. He is quiet but good-humored, well liked by many. He is a very large man, tall and broad, and he has a certain gentleness that tempers his size. His wife is devoted to him and he to her."

"Such a paragon! If I were your Silas, I would be jealous."

She could see by the flush on his pale skin that he was sorry for the words the moment he said them, for crossing the boundary that made their friendship possible. She didn't want him to feel sorry or awkward, and so she answered without reserve.

"No, if you were my Silas, you would be infinitely relieved. General Washington is more than a capable man, he is a promise that other colonies will fight with us. I will sleep easier knowing that Silas and my brothers have him to command them, to hold their lives dear, as I do."

Willfully she crossed the boundary, too. Not wanting to jar his wounded right side, she took his left hand and cradled it in both of hers. "I wish things were not as they are. Under other circumstances, you and Silas might have been good friends. Under other circumstances, you would find General Washington a worthy man to know. Like them, you are intelligent, reasonable, and kind. It is the worst tragedy of this time that men who are so alike must be enemies."

"You are very wise in some ways, but naive in others," he told her. "Silas and I would never be aught but rivals, no matter what the political situation." The look in his eyes belied the smile that made light of his words. She was flattered, but she retreated into safety and ignored his meaning.

"I wish I knew a worthy young woman—of Tory sympathies, of course—to introduce to Captain Byrne," she said to Sarah. "He's a fine man."

"Yes, he is, despite his loyalties," Sarah conceded, "but I don't think there's time... That is, surely you can see..."

Sarah looked so sad and sympathetic, Addie could not mistake her meaning.

"You and Tullia, you are ready to bury him before his time! He's getting better! All of the men brought to us are healing, including Captain Byrne!"

"You must be right. You know far more about these things than I," Sarah said apologetically, but her eyes did not meet Addie's until she changed the subject to General Washington. "You are certain he has arrived? You are sure he will be a good commander?"

"Yes and yes. The British are all astir about it. If they say that 'Mr.' Washington arrived yesterday, then he did. And I know he is the best man to lead our army." Patiently she repeated all the good things she had already told Captain Byrne about him. Sarah did not know him personally and was desperate to believe that Justin would be well commanded.

Addie tried not to hover over Captain Byrne, but she found herself back at his bedside in the late afternoon. He was sleeping, and she sat beside the bed, watching the faint motion of his breathing. She wanted to deny the truth, but suddenly, it wasn't possible any longer. Tullia and Sarah were right. He wasn't recovering; he was drifting away.

Sometime later, his eyelids fluttered and then his eyes opened. But at first, when he looked at her, there was no recognition in his eyes. Then he managed a smile. "I was in England, with my family. I could see them so clearly. I could even smell the perfume from the roses and lavender in the garden."

"You will be there again," Addie said, knowing it was not true.

Aside from a sip of water, he didn't want anything, and he was soon asleep again, but still she stayed. When Tullia came to check on her, Addie left the room only long enough to explain. "I cannot leave him, not tonight. This is something I must do. Please explain to Sarah and Papa for me."

Tullia opened her mouth to protest, saw the resolution in Addie, and said, "I'll be nearby. You call if you need me."

Addie lost track of time. All of her energy was concentrated on willing Paul Byrne to live. But she heard the difference when his breathing changed, becoming more labored. As soft as the candlelight was, his face was cast in harsh relief, so gaunt he scarcely resembled the man she had known before the battle.

His eyes opened, and he looked directly at her, but the faint word he spoke was "Mother?"

She didn't question her instinct; she climbed up onto the high bed beside him, and with infinite care, she cradled his head against her breast. "Yes, my dear. You are home and safe. All is well. You may rest now."

His eyes closed. He drew one more long, rasping breath, and then he was gone. She felt him leave as if he had gotten up and walked from the room, and she hoped that in his last moments, he had been home in the England he had loved enough to gift with his life.

Addie began to weep, more in rage than in sorrow. It was such a waste that this special man had died. It was a waste that others had and more would in this war. She believed in the right of colonists to be governed fairly, but that right seemed vague and unreachable in contrast to the cold death in her arms.

Tullia came to her, having kept watch. Her strong hands pulled Addie away from the corpse. "You've done all there was to do for him. He's gone to the Lord now, away from here."

"I hope he went to England first," Addie sobbed, not caring if it sounded mad.

The next days passed in a haze, but Addie was grateful to her father for arranging that Captain Byrne be buried in King's Chapel with a fine marble marker. He said it was the least he could do as Callista had recommended the young man to them. But Addie knew that in large part his generosity was for her because she had cared about the captain in spite of her loyalty to the Rebels.

The captain's fellow officers went out of their way to thank Addie for her care of their friend, and their gratitude made her feel uncomfortable, as if she were a fraud. They assumed she was as loyal to the Crown as Captain Byrne had been, as they themselves were. One of them presented her with the captain's signet ring, saying, "He asked that I give this to you if he died. He cared deeply about you, Mistress Valencourt."

She did not refuse the ring. One did not question the wishes of the dying. And she was glad to have something tangible to hold against the shock of having Captain Byrne so irrevocably gone.

Captain Byrne was Silas and her brothers. She didn't want it to be so, but in her nightmares, the captain at his moment of death became one of the others. And most of the time, that other was Silas. Again and again, she awakened herself with her own sobbing and the crying of his name.

She was no longer sure that staying in Boston was the right thing to do. She was missing days with Silas. That might not matter if both of them were fated to live to old age, but the captain's death had made her face the fact that there was no promise of that in normal times and much less in war.

She discussed it with Sarah, asking, "Do you still think of leaving?"

"Every day, but my obligation to my parents remains, and more, though I know the redcoats make much of our army's difficulties, it is probably true that the encampment remains too disorganized to make it a fit place for the men's families."

Addie had heard the same reports, accounts of the soldiers being so filthy that their smallclothes rotted on their bodies and General Washington having to issue orders regarding bathing and personal cleanliness. The men were accustomed to their womenfolk keeping their clothing and abodes clean, and they hadn't reckoned on being obliged to do domestic chores while they were defending their political rights. At present, the only women Washington needed in camp were laundresses.

Addie's shoulders slumped in defeat. "I have the same obligations. I worry about Mary. She is somewhat improved, but she continues poorly. My father is very concerned about her, and Peter and Jane fret because their mother has so little energy for them. And if Silas and my brothers wanted us to come to them, they would find a means to tell us so."

With their Patriot sympathies, it wasn't becoming any easier for the two women to remain in the town. With their questionable victory at Breed's Hill, the British seemed to have lost all patience with the opposition and, in their frustration, they sought to defile Patriot symbols.

The Old South Meeting House, because it had served as a Rebel gathering place as well as a place of worship, was treated most shamefully. The pulpit was torn down, the high-sided box pews broken up for kindling, and tons of dirt were smoothed over the floor to create a space for equestrian displays as the building was transformed into an officers' club and a riding academy. Liquor was dispensed in the gallery, and the Queen's Light Dragoons rode their mounts round and round.

In another direct insult, plans were made to form an amateur theatrical company with officers and their ladies playing the major parts. The Puritan heart of Boston had not only disdained the frivolity of theater, it had long since passed laws against plays being performed, though many people read them.

Even Marcus, who did not frown on such pursuits, was uneasy with this flagrant disregard for local custom and law. "They are behaving as if there were no Congregationalists among the Loyalists, but that is not true. His Majesty's forces should be more gracious in dealing with the peculiarities of this place." This was a great concession from Marcus given that he had always regretted that theater was not allowed in Boston.

Many of the problems facing the city were much more basic than those of cultural conflict. As the warmth of summer gave way to the chill of autumn and winter, firewood and other essentials grew scarce. The redcoats thought nothing of chopping down the graceful trees that lined the Common. They broke down fences and scavenged wood from old buildings. The gardens had provided fresh vegetables and fruit in summer, as well as some supplies for winter, but not nearly enough for everyone in Boston. Salt meat and dried beans and peas became the usual fare, and the health of many suffered as a result. The enlisted men and their families were the hardest hit because their meager wages allowed for little extra food, even were it available. British supply ships were being taken at sea by privateering Patriot vessels, and when the ships did manage to get through with provisions, most were sold at public auction, that being deemed the fairest method of distribution, though it was of little use to the poor.

Because of Tullia's skill and determination, the Valencourt household was as well supplied as any could be in a city under siege. But she fretted because there were still soldiers visiting with them, and that meant extra mouths to feed. For their part, the officers brought what they could, but their offerings were often foods Tullia did not wish to serve, nor would she deny them the healthier fare from her larder.

The Valencourts had their milk cow and a small flock of chickens, but Tullia worried about feed for the livestock over the winter. Everyone in the city who had beasts to feed had the same worry. Boston, with its rope walks for the manufacture of cordage used mainly on ships, with its docks, wharves, and warehouses, was a seaport town dependent on the outlying farms and forests for the bounty of the land. Denied that bounty, the city was rapidly slipping from its position as a prosperous port of trade to a starving backwater.

Marcus pretended that business was going on normally, and Addie still went frequently with him to the shops, but trade was much diminished, and income was down from the rents ordinarily paid to him from wharfage and other commercial properties. Darius managed to have some merchandise shipped to his father, but, as Quentin had predicted, there simply wasn't much room for books, paper, and such on British transports. Marcus had begun to offer volumes from his library for sale, and they were quickly purchased by officers who were bored with garrison duty.

It saddened Addie to see the books disappearing from the shelves because she knew how precious they were to her father. But she realized that the pretense that life was somehow going to go on as it always had was more valuable to him. When he was home, he spent most of his time with Mary and the children, and even in this, there was a touch of desperation. Addie knew that Mary saw it, too, and she was grateful for her stepmother's patience. Mary's pregnancy continued to sap her strength, but she did not complain, speaking only of her eagerness to meet this new child. Addie did not want to consider that Mary might not survive childbirth this time, but the thought was never far from her mind.

Mary went into labor a week before Christmas, alarming every adult in the house except for Mary herself. As if in compensation for the trials of the previous months, the actual delivery was swift and comparatively easy, and Marcus was presented with a new daughter, Letitia.

Marcus had named all of his children in tribute to the Latin and Greek classics that had absorbed so many hours of his life and brought him such contentment. But Letitia, meaning "joyful" in Latin, was a particularly poignant choice for the times, as if this small scrap of humanity could somehow turn the tide of war's sorrow.

Addie was deeply touched when the officers who had most often visited the house presented the new parents with a silver cup for Letitia.

When she showed it to her sister-in-law, Sarah handled it gingerly, shaking her head. "I don't want to like them. They are the enemy. But they do make it difficult to hate them. My parents were at their wits' end to replace servants who fled. Now they have a sergeant and his wife, the Browns, living with them and doing an enormous amount of work because they are so grateful to have pleasant living quarters.

I confess, I worry less about my parents because the Browns are with them, and I have guilt for feeling so."

"You must know that Justin would understand," Addie said. "Anything that makes this time easier for you would meet with his approval."

"I am not sure any more what Justin would or would not understand." Sarah's voice trembled. "Sometimes the days of our marriage seem like a dream, as if they never happened at all. He is such a short distance away, but he might as well be in another country. I look at Letitia, and I long for Justin's child, for proof of our life together."

Addie understood Sarah's complaint too well. Though she thought of Silas every day, something had changed. She no longer hungered physically for him. He had slipped back into the place he had occupied before she had become aware of him as a desirable man. It was an unsettling shift that could only be resolved by seeing him again. And though she didn't point it out to Sarah, for all they knew, the men might be farther away than that short distance. There were rumors that some of the Continental Army had invaded Canada and were hoping to bring those provinces in on the Patriots' side.

"'Semper in absentes felicior aestus amantes,'" Addie quoted wryly. "'Absence makes the heart grow fonder.' If he believed that, maybe old Sextus Propertius didn't love his Cynthia as much as he claimed." And she confessed how distant she felt from Silas.

"Well, I shall just go on with my studies and will know that much more for the delay in seeing Justin again," Sarah said, determined to lighten their depression.

Addie thought of how intolerable life would be if she did not have Sarah's friendship to sustain her.

Neither of them looked forward to spending Christmas without the men, particularly in this year when the traditional feasting of Anglican households would be curtailed by food and fuel shortages. But on the day of Christmas Eve, Sarah found Addie at home, and suddenly the ice of winter seemed miraculously thawed.

Addie knew Sarah had word from Justin even before Sarah handed the paper to her and whispered, "This time the messenger found me.

He must have been watching the house, poor lad. He gave me this and was gone before I could offer him any refreshment against the cold."

They were all well, including Quentin. They sent their love, and Justin included special words for Sarah, while Silas again committed himself openly to Addie: "My dearest, I am in a fever of impatience, waiting for the day when we can be together. Be of good heart. I love you."

So few words, and yet Addie felt her blood quicken as Silas's image filled her until it was almost as if he stood before her, and she could see the strong planes of his face, the lean height of him, could feel the clever, long-fingered hands touching her.

Addie touched her cheeks, feeling the heat there. "I take back what I said about Sextus Propertius. It seems being apart from me has been a sharp spur to Silas's desire, and I was too quick to judge that mine for him had vanished," she admitted, and then the two women were laughing unrestrainedly for the pure joy of being alive and young and in love.

When they finally sobered, Addie said, "This time I think I must tell Papa. He never mentions them, but I know he worries."

Sarah shrugged. "Perhaps you are right. Having a new baby here must make your father think of other children who are not with him. And as we don't know who the messengers are or how they enter and leave the city, we could scarcely betray them even were we questioned."

"Papa will not betray us either." Addie was suddenly sure of that.

Christmas dinner was meager, with two scrawny chickens as the main dish, but Tullia tried to make it better for the children by serving some of her precious plum jelly made in the summer when fruit and sugar had been available. And the officers who shared the meal with them brought fine Madeira and a pineapple from the West Indies. The exotic fruit, symbol of hospitality, was a special treat in the best of times, but in the present straitened circumstances, it was a lavish gift.

Addie waited until the festivities were over before she sought a few moments alone with her father.

"I have a gift for you. At least, I hope that is how you will regard it. Sarah and I have had news of my brothers and Silas. They are in good health, and they send their love. Before your suspicions are aroused,

I assure you we don't know who brought the message or how to send word in return."

He stared impassively at her for a long moment, and then his face crumpled and he moaned, a low sound of pain that tore at her heart. He covered his face with his hands, and his shoulders heaved as he wept. "I do not understand their treason. I will never understand it! But I love them still. I do not want them to suffer or to die. I think of them every day."

Addie went to where he sat at his desk, and she put her arms around him. "I know they think of you, too, Papa. Their love is as constant as yours."

Her father was so torn, Addie doubted the wisdom of having told him about the message. But then she felt him straightening his bowed shoulders, collecting himself, and his voice had steadied when he said, "I did not think anything could gladden my heart in this dark time more than seeing Mary safely delivered of our child. But knowing that my sons and Silas have not perished is equal to that joy. Thank you, Addie, for your gift."

For a small space of time, Addie felt as close to her father as she ever had, but then she remembered all that separated them and kept her brothers and Silas from this house even at Christmas.

The first month of the new year did not allow Addie to believe that 1776 was going to bring a peaceful resolution to their lives. The redcoats had gone ahead with their theatrical plans, but the performance at Faneuil Hall on January 8 was interrupted by a Rebel attack on Charlestown. The firing could be heard clearly in Boston, many thought the attack was on the Neck, and the crowd in the theater panicked; the officers and soldiers tried to get out to join their regiments while some of the women in the audience shrieked and fainted, adding to the general chaos.

The Rebels took some prisoners and burned some British quarters in Charlestown, but Addie thought their disruption of the opening night of a specially written farce entitled "The Blockade of Boston" was a better victory.

Other events were not so amusing. Word came from England that in October, when Parliament had opened its session at Westminster, the King had issued an address from the throne making it clear that his policy would be to suppress the rebellion in America but that mercy would be shown if the Rebels repented. The King had rejected utterly the colonies' petitions for reconciliation through more just governing. It was growing impossible to pretend that the King did not know or did not approve of the policies formulated by his ministers and Parliament.

General Gage had returned to England in October to give an account of himself to Lord North, and he had left General Howe in charge. General Clinton was also part of the hierarchy, and when he sailed south with two companies of light infantry, it was certain that he intended mischief somewhere, but his plans remained secret. Addie hoped he did not mean to attack in Virginia.

And things were getting worse in Boston as both the occupying army and the civilian residents found it increasingly difficult to obtain enough food to eat and fuel to keep warm. Addie felt as if they were all holding their breath, waiting for the Patriot forces to attack the city or for the redcoats to venture out against General Washington—or waiting until the city perished from hunger and disease. Fevers, chest complaints, dysentery, and worst of all, smallpox, were claiming more victims by the day.

"Bad food makes bad sickness," Tullia muttered over and over until Addie was tempted to remind her that repeating that particular truth was not likely to put good food on the table.

If there was little food for the body, there was an ample feast for the mind, depending on one's political loyalties. A pamphlet entitled *Common Sense, written by an Englishman who has been in the colonies for only two years*, was causing a great furor. Marcus labeled it "seditious." Addie thought it glorious, though she did not tell her father that. The ideas were not new, but Thomas Paine had stated them with clear strength. Government was necessary to restrain lawlessness, but its power came from its citizens, not from a monarchy. He claimed that only harm could come to America through continued political attachment to England. He cried out for nothing less than full independence for America.

Addie could imagine her brothers and Silas reading the pamphlet and feeling renewed hope in the justness of their cause, even as the British authorities despaired of stopping the dissemination of the document. She wanted to discuss it with Sarah and went in search of her. Mistress Goodwin had been ailing, so Addie had not seen Sarah for several days. She checked at Sarah's house first and was told Sarah had been staying with her parents these past days and nights.

She felt no disquiet until Sarah's housekeeper shook her head and muttered, "She 'asn't sent for extra clothing. She 'asn't sent no word at all, not even orders for us. That's not like 'er. The mistress is that careful of 'er 'ouse. She wants everything in order when the master comes 'ome."

Addie assured the woman that Sarah trusted her to keep the household running smoothly in her absence and that she would undoubtedly send word or return shortly. The woman preened visibly at this expression of confidence; she had been hired by Justin and Sarah right before they married, and she was proud enough of her position that it made no difference to her whether the redcoats or the Rebels controlled Boston.

Despite her placating words to the housekeeper, Addie hastened her steps toward the Goodwin house. Sarah's mother must be very ill for Sarah to so neglect her own household. Not until she was faced with the reality of it did Addie consider that Sarah herself might be ill also, and then all thought of political tracts fled from her mind.

Sarah's father had had smallpox in his youth, but her mother had not, nor had Sarah. Now they were sick, as was Sergeant Brown. The few other servants who had worked in the house had fled, leaving Mistress Brown and Mr. Goodwin to care for the stricken three.

Addie's terror was so great, she was paralyzed with it, and then her heart calmed because there was no choice. She wrote a brief account of what was happening, assuring her father she would return home when she could. She cautioned him not to send anyone to her. Letitia had not been inoculated against the pox yet, and she did not want to risk infecting her. She could not recall that Sarah had been with the baby in recent days, when she might have passed the disease to her, but there was nothing to be done about it anyway.

She collared a ragged boy, gave him the message, instructions, and a coin, with the promise of another when he returned with a note from her father. She wanted to begin tending Sarah immediately, but she forced herself to wait until the boy returned so that she would not endanger him either.

"God keep you and Sarah safe," Marcus had written. "I will make sure clothing for you and food for all are delivered to the Goodwin house."

Mr. Goodwin bore little resemblance to the energetic merchant Addie had known. He had become a gray-faced old man, crushed by the horror of what was happening to his family and by his own guilt. "I could have had them inoculated, as your father did his own, but I was afraid they would die of it. Now they will die without it."

"Mr. Goodwin, we don't know that. Many survive the disease. If you will care for your wife, and Mistress Brown for her husband, I will see to Sarah, and together we will give them the best care possible."

Mr. Goodwin and Mistress Brown deferred to her as if she had always been head of this house, and Addie accepted the role because she did not see an alternative. Her father was true to his word, sending the clothing and having food as well as firewood delivered daily. She made sure Mr. Goodwin and Mistress Brown ate and that nourishing broth was available for the sick whenever they could be coaxed to drink it. She hauled water for everyone's needs and kept enough fires going to prevent the sickrooms from growing too chilled. She did all the chores and hardly noticed her aching muscles because she was concentrating entirely on Sarah.

As she had told Mr. Goodwin, so Addie kept reminding herself that smallpox was not always fatal. The marks of it were on many people, including Silas, who had faint tracings on his left cheek. And though she had never seen a full-blown case, she knew that the disease had different manifestations, mild in some, severe but passing in others, fatal for the unfortunate.

Sarah was so feverish, at first she didn't understand that Addie was with her. She talked to Justin, showing him things in their house, welcoming him home.

"He'll be here someday soon," Addie assured her over and over as she bathed her hot skin.

It was almost worse when Sarah was conscious. "Justin wanted me to be inoculated, but my father has always feared the practice. It is the smallpox, I know. How are my mother and Sergeant Brown?"

"They are recovering," Addie said, though she wasn't sure, "and so will you."

Sarah peered at her hands and touched her face. "No sores yet, but they will come, won't they? Poor Justin, he will have to bear with a scarred wife. Perhaps I shall smooth my skin with beeswax, and then I shall have to keep my distance from the hearth, else my false skin will melt." Though tears stood in her eyes, she giggled at that; the fever had made her giddy.

"You may escape with no marks at all," Addie said. "But even if you don't, Justin will care for nothing except that you are safe. Silas has scars, but they are no stop to me. Why, even General Washington is marked."

Sarah's eyes grew glassier, and she plucked restlessly at the bedclothes. "I thought Justin was here. It seemed as if he was. How very odd."

"Sarah, he could be here. I am sure Papa could arrange it with the authorities so that Justin could be given permission to come to you. The British are not monsters." Addie hadn't planned to suggest this to her sister-in-law, but as she did, she was convinced it was possible,

But Sarah would have none of it. "No! You must promise me you will not arrange it! Promise! I don't want Justin to see me like this. I don't want him to be in the redcoats' power."

Sarah was growing so agitated, Addie gave her word, and there was guilt in the relief she felt because she wasn't really sure of what the redcoats would do were Justin in their grasp, even if they had issued a pass. And she understood Sarah not wanting Justin to see her when she was so afflicted; Addie would not want Silas brought to her were she in the same position. She promised herself that Sarah was going to recover. Captain Byrne had died, so Sarah must live. It made perfect sense to her.

But when the rash appeared on Sarah's skin, it showed the spreading blotches of hemorrhage, and Addie recognized that as the worst possible sign. Still, she refused to believe Sarah would be lost to her. Her ferocious care of her was as selfish as anything she had ever done. Sarah had become so important to her, she would not let her go. She was not repulsed by the stench or the blood or anything at all about the disease because the Sarah she loved was captive to these demons, and she would free her, for herself, for Justin, and most of all, for Sarah herself who was so full of life and so determined to learn everything that she might hold Justin's love even after her beauty had faded.

The disease raged, consuming Sarah's small body, burning away her flesh, bleeding away her life. The last time she was conscious, she looked straight at Addie. Her voice was only a wisp of sound, but Addie heard every word. "You take care of him for me. Promise?"

And Addie promised.

Sarah died early one cold morning before the sun rose.

Addie sat with the body, waiting for the sun, judging that dawn would be soon enough to tell the rest of the household. She thought very carefully about what must be done to lay Sarah to rest, but she felt nothing, not grief, not rage, nothing at all. Even her body felt numb, so that she had to will herself to move one step at a time when she finally went to inform Sarah's father of the death.

Mr. Goodwin blinked owlishly at her and nodded, no more capable than she of expressing any emotion.

Mistress Brown was not so reticent. Her husband was indeed recovering, and though Mrs. Goodwin was very weak, it seemed she would survive, too. But Sarah was dead, and Mistress Brown had no doubt that her husband had brought the infection into the house because everyone knew the disease traveled with the army, and there were cases in the Boston garrison.

"We meant 'em no 'arm," she sobbed. "They been good to us, makin' our lot so much better."

"Mistress Brown, there is no way to prove whether or not Sergeant Brown brought the disease into this house. It does not signify anyway. No deliberate harm was intended, whatever the case may be, so there is no guilt or blame in this. You have worked hard for the Goodwins and eased their way as much as they have yours. And there is work yet to do." Addie gave the woman detailed instructions, including the order to burn all the clothing she herself would leave behind, Sarah's bedding, and that of the two other patients. "Until they are completely recovered, what comes in contact with them must be destroyed so that no healthy person is infected by matter left on the cloth. I am going home, but I will request my father's aid in arranging for Sarah's burial. It must be discreetly done."

She felt like a very old woman as she plodded homeward, but when she reached the house, she was careful, enlisting Tullia's help so that she could strip off all of her clothing and scrub down before she entered the house. The look of shock on Tullia's normally calm face told her how awful she looked, but she didn't have the energy to reassure her. It took all of her concentration to stay on her feet until she explained to her father and Tullia.

"Sarah died this morning. Her mother and Sergeant Brown are recovering. The household will still need food and other help, and, Papa, arrangements must be made to bury Sarah and to take care of her house." She pressed her fingers to her temples, trying to remember anything else that might need to be done, but a dark fog was rolling over her, and she wasn't strong enough to hold on to the light.

Dimly she knew she was being half led, half carried to her bed and that Tullia was assuring Marcus that it was exhaustion not disease.

The last thing she heard was Tullia soothing her. "Sleep now, child. You did all you could." Tullia's work-roughened hand stroked her forehead with infinite gentleness, but Addie drifted in a gray place beyond solace.

Chapter 10

Spring 1776

There were rumors that the Rebels had hauled guns from Fort Ticonderoga, some three hundred miles away, to Cambridge. There were also rumors that the Rebels were going to invade Boston by boat or that Howe was going to attack the Rebels by the same means. Addie paid little attention to any of it. Her mind remained locked away in the sorrow of Sarah's death, her body in the grip of exhaustion. When she tried to eat or sleep, she saw Sarah's ravaged body and heard her fevered ramblings. She could smell the stench of the disease.

But she could not ignore the boom of cannon on the night of March 2, as the newly acquired American artillery fired on the Neck and British guns answered. However, morning revealed the attack had been a diversion, the noise and action there covering the sounds of hundreds of men and trundling carts heading for Dorchester Heights, blanketing the sounds of the men digging in so that by morning they were well established on the ground that commanded the southern part of town and would enable them to fire on British ships and the city, as well as to cut off communication between the main garrison and the British outworks on the Neck.

Fortune had smiled on the Patriots, giving them a mild moonlit night for their work but adding a low-lying fog that had hidden them from British eyes. They had even been able to relieve the first work parties with fresh men at three in the morning without drawing attention to their activities. They had compensated for the hard ground and difficult digging by bringing in bundles of twisted straw, and by filling barrels with dirt and rocks, to add to their barricades. Further, they had felled trees and sharpened the ends, setting them with points out to impede any enemy advance.

By March 4, the fortifications were so extensive, the British were amazed.

Many of Captain Byrne's friends continued to visit the Valencourts and were concerned about Addie's state since Sarah's death. They usually tried to offer some cheerful topic, but the new fortifications were too impressive to ignore.

"One of our engineers claims that no fewer than fifteen or twenty thousand men could have accomplished so much in such a short time, which means that Mr. Washington's army must be very large, indeed," one officer said.

"Or else the works were raised by magic," another offered. "That must be it! Two posts raised on the heights in two days, two places from which to fire on us and defend themselves—only magic will answer how it was done."

Addie refrained from reminding them that the Patriots had proven themselves fast workmen before the Battle of Bunker Hill. Interest stirred through her lethargy, and suddenly, she longed desperately to see her brothers and Silas. Then she remembered that when she saw them, Justin would learn of Sarah's death.

Most expected the British would attack on March 5, the fifth anniversary of the Boston Massacre, and in a hastily planned attempt, Howe tried to do just that. But no one in Boston, including General Howe, had any control over the elements. He embarked troops on boats, but a raging storm struck, whipping the water in the harbor to such frenzy, no boats could cross. More than one person muttered that Howe was probably grateful for the storm. The British position in Boston grew more untenable by the day, and by launching an attack, Howe might lose a great deal more than he could afford and gain nothing. Nor was it possible to overlook the fact that he could have fortified Dorchester Heights himself long before the Rebels claimed the high ground.

The news that Howe would evacuate Boston brought pleas from citizens, no matter what their political beliefs, that he not burn the city. It was a strong counter to wager and was accepted by Washington—if allowed to leave without hindrance the British would not destroy the city.

But while leaving without being fired upon might solve one of Howe's greatest worries, it did nothing to help him with the problem of the Loyalists who wanted to leave with him. There were hundreds of them, and General Howe was too much of a gentleman to leave behind any who wished to go. Arranging transport for them was a major undertaking.

Marcus knew he had to take his family and leave. He and his newspaper had been too outspoken on behalf of the Loyalist cause, and his association with high-ranking British officers was well known. But he wanted to believe that their absence would be only temporary, just until the rebellion was over and the King's authority restored.

Feeling it would be useless, Addie did not argue with him, but to her surprise, Mary did.

"Whatever may happen in the future, you must prepare as if we're leaving forever. You have extensive holdings here; you cannot trust that they will be intact if and when we return. And you must provide for those of your children who will not be coming with us. No matter what your differences with them, you must not leave them impoverished in such precarious times."

Marcus was sharing a scant supper with his wife and daughter during this exchange, and he was taken aback by Mary's firm defiance. He stared at her in consternation, and then his gaze swung to Addie.

"You will, of course, be coming with us?"

"No, I won't," she said. "I will be waiting for my brothers and Silas to enter the city, and I will marry Silas as soon as possible. I hope we will have your blessing. I love you, Papa, but my life is in this country. I think you are mistaken. I believe this rebellion is a true revolution that will not end until we hold our destiny in our hands." For the first time since Sarah's death, she felt a surge of emotion.

He did not rail at her; grief and resignation etched his features. "I cannot do battle with both my wife and my daughter. The world is changing too swiftly for me, and I am too old to change with it. I cannot make you a prisoner and carry you away with us. I will fear for you, but I must trust that Silas will care well for you and you for him. As much as I am able, I will arrange matters to your benefit. Now, if you will excuse me."

He left them, and the silence stretched between them until Addie said, "Thank you, Mary, for your concern, but I do not want Papa to take from you and your children to provide for us."

"He won't do that," Mary said. "Despite the refusal of his heart to accept what is happening, his mind has been far more sensible for a long time. His credit is strong with his London bankers. Wherever we go, he will be able to take care of us. And if we go to England, Callista, her husband, and other connections of your father's will be there for us."

"This is very difficult for you, isn't it?" Addie studied the soft beauty of her stepmother's face. "You are as much a Patriot as I, yet you must leave."

"Addie, there is sorrow, but I go with a glad heart. You must believe that. It is a question of loyalty, as is so much of life. My loyalty is to your father. I admire and love him, and he is father to all of my children, as much to Peter and Jane as to Clement and Letitia. Trust me to cherish him as you and Silas will cherish each other." She paused and tears glittered in her eyes. "You and your brothers, but most of all you, will have my gratitude forever. You could have made it very difficult for me to marry Marcus. You could have made this house an intolerable place to be. But you did not. You accepted me as your father's choice, and you welcomed my children, making them feel as if this had always been their home. I pray God will watch over all of you and keep you safe."

"There was no choice to make," Addie assured her. "You made Papa happy, and that was enough for all of us."

It was the last peaceful interlude. Though Howe had promised not to destroy the city, that did not stop the pillaging of anything that might be of use to the Rebels when they arrived. There was also plundering out of sheer greed. Marcus had to pay a man two dollars a day to guard Justin's house, but he did it. It was harsh enough that his son would return to find his wife had died, let alone to face the additional wound of a ruined house. Marcus also paid the servants who were still there to stay. They had remained because they hadn't known what to do when informed that their mistress had died, and they were grateful to have a position for at least a while longer.

Sarah's parents, in spite of her mother's frailty, would leave, and Marcus did what he could to ease their way since both of them seemed to have been rendered incapable by the tragedy that had struck them.

For all Marcus's will that even this extreme disaster be conducted with some order, life in Boston grew increasingly chaotic. People were informed when space had been allotted to them on a ship, and once that word came, there was little time before boarding. Nor was anyone sure of where they were going, except away from Boston. With so many leaving the city, quarters on the vessels were very cramped, and Howe had issued orders that furnishings for which there was no room would be dumped. Soon, the harbor was awash with exquisite chairs, tables, cabinets, and other valuable pieces, and there were piles of the same in the streets where the owners had abandoned them.

When word came for the Valencourts, Addie accompanied them to the wharf. They had trunks and bundles with them, but most of Marcus's prized possessions remained in the house, the house and contents he had deeded to Addie and her brothers.

The commercial properties he had transferred to Darius, in the hope there would be safety in having his son in New York claim ownership and thus preserve the book and print shops, the wharfage, and other business-based acreage and buildings. At least Mary had persuaded him to store the press, type, and other printing equipment in one of his warehouses, to make them less obvious targets for vandals.

Darius was as outspoken a Loyalist as Marcus, and Addie could not see how he would be able to deal with property under Patriot control, but given the circumstances, she thought their father was being generous to leave the house to her and her brothers.

Tullia saw the travelers off from the house. There was no question of her going into exile with them, though Marcus had assured her that he would always have a position for her, no matter where he and Mary settled.

Tullia had thanked him politely and declined. "I came with Mistress Lily. I will stay with her children for as long as they need me."

"Thank you, Tullia. My heart will rest easier knowing that," he had told her.

But now, at the moment of parting, he looked at the woman and thought of Lily, of how much he had loved her, of the bright beautiful children they had created together. And though he did not want to face it, he suffered a growing conviction that he might never see Tullia or Lily's children again.

Beyond words, he nodded his head at Tullia, and she acknowledged him in the same way, her dark eyes luminous with tears she did not allow herself to shed.

Addie welcomed the confusion of the scene at the wharf, the cacophony of voices, the push and shove of knots of people trying to sort out themselves and their belongings. She welcomed the now familiar numbness that made it feel as though all of it were happening at some remove from herself.

But then there was no more time, and the reality of the moment hit her with full force.

"Why aren't you coming with us?" Jane demanded, her little face puckered with worry. She was not yet six years old, but she knew this was not like other partings.

Addie swallowed hard before she trusted her voice. "I have to wait here because our brothers and Silas will be coming home soon. They would be sad if no one were here to greet them. And even if you and I can't be together for a while, we can write letters to each other." She wasn't certain that letters could be exchanged, but it was the best she could offer.

Jane thought this over before she said, "If Mama and Papa help me, I can write them letters."

Peter was only two years older than Jane, but in understanding he was far more mature. He looked up at Addie. "Tell my brothers and Silas that I hope they will be happy. Tell them I will miss them. And I will miss you, too, Addie." Despite his best efforts, his face crumpled, and Addie knelt down to draw both children into her arms.

"If you think of this as a grand adventure, and make many notes and draw pictures, you will remember everything so that you can tell your children stories when you are all grown up." Then she whispered, "Since I can't go with you, I know you'll take care of Mama and Papa and the babies." She straightened, willing herself not to weep in front of Peter and Jane.

She and Mary embraced briefly, Mary murmuring, "Don't worry about us. We will be all right." Holding Letitia in her arms and overseeing the woman who was caring for Clement, she shepherded Peter and Jane away so that Addie and Marcus were left alone.

Father and daughter regarded each other solemnly, both of them made reticent by the fear of being overcome by their emotions. But Addie realized she was more afraid that they would simply nod at each other as her father and Tullia had done. She needed more than that from him, wanted to give him more.

She put her arms around him. Like all of them, he had grown leaner over the winter months, and his face was more lined, his hair showed much more silver than it had just a year ago. But to Addie, he was still a commanding figure, this tall, strong man who had always tempered his edicts with reason, had always tried to order his domain with as much kindness as logic, and who had recognized and encouraged the individuality of each of his children. In Addie herself, in all of Lily's children, that encouragement that he had given to their minds had, in the end, carried them away from his own beliefs, away from him. Addie felt his arms come around to hold her as tightly as she held him.

"Thank you, Papa, thank you for everything," she murmured, hoping he would understand. "I love you."

Marcus was true to his word. Not even to protect her would he force her to go with him into exile. He knew he had lost her to the rebellion as completely as he had lost his sons to the Rebel army. And in that instant, he also knew he would not change a single thing about this beloved daughter.

"Even now, Addie, even now I am proud of you and of your brothers and Silas," he said, his voice cracking under the strain. "I will hold all of you in my heart, forever. Tell them for me."

His arms dropped away from her, and she let him go, watching until he had rejoined Mary and the children. Addie opened her hand in a gesture of farewell, and she turned away, blinded by tears, unable to watch any longer. She had heard the unspoken words clearly; her father was no longer insisting they would be back soon, or at all.

Chapter 11

It had been less than a year since Ad, his brothers, and Silas had left Boston, but to all of them, it seemed much longer than that. The Valencourts missed their family, and Justin was wild to return to Sarah, Silas to be reunited with Addie. But they were apprehensive about Marcus, and Sarah's father. Staunch Loyalists such as they were unlikely to stay in the town, but nonetheless, it was hard to imagine two men who had established their fortunes there leaving everything behind.

All Silas could think of was that if they were leaving on the ships, their families would be going with them, and to him, that meant Addie. Her brothers assured him she would not go, but he doubted that his brief avowals of devotion or even her patriotism would weigh heavily enough to keep her in place while Marcus, Mary, and the children sailed away. He knew it was useless to dwell upon it, but he could not help wishing for the umpteenth time that he had forsaken his lofty ideas of honor and married Addie before the war began. In his worst moments of doubt, he imagined that she had succumbed to the charm of a redcoat, most probably Captain Byrne, and was preparing to leave with not only her family, but also her husband. He and her brothers had sent word twice, but they had had no way of receiving news in return.

Ad knew Addie was waiting. He knew his twin too well to believe she would leave with the Loyalists, though one of those might be their father. But he was anxious to get to her, to make sure she was well.

"We will be in the city soon."

Ad started at the sound of General Washington's voice. "Yes, Your Excellency."

"I would that we were sure of Howe's intentions. The city of New York would seem his logical destination, but we have no proof of that, only speculation."

Ad waited patiently and then began to pen the orders the General dictated, orders that, as soon as the British were out of Boston, would begin sending units of the Continental Army on the long march south to confront Howe's forces if they came ashore in New York.

General Washington had warmly welcomed the Valencourts, pleased to see familiar faces in the sea of strangers. The General could make Justin and Ad members of his personal staff without seeming to favor Virginians, because the Valencourts were perceived as Massachusetts men and as such strong Patriots they had defied their Loyalist father to join first the militia and then the Continental Army. Of course, some viewed the Loyalist connection with alarm and suspicion, but Washington chose to ignore them.

Ad had long admired Washington as an affable, intelligent man, but serving as one of his aides-de-camp, he was astonished daily by how astute the general was as he sought to forge one strong army from all the disparate units from the various colonies. It was not easy, for men who were together because they had chosen to rebel against the established order of government were not apt to take orders docilely, especially from their peers. It sat ill with them to have to defer to someone who had been no higher in the social order than they before the war. But Washington understood that without discipline, without respect, and even some fear of their officers and of disobeying commands, common soldiers could not be relied upon to hold steady under fire from the British Army. When he had arrived at Cambridge, he had moved swiftly to curtail fraternizing between officers and their men and to establish order by instituting severe punishments ranging from flogging to hanging, depending on the nature of the crime. And even with his aides-de-camp and the guards assigned to protect him, Washington maintained the formal mien of a commanding officer.

Ad thought the general must find his role very lonely sometimes, but he did not resent the change. He saw the necessity of it.

Ad was honored that Washington had found him worthy to serve as one of his secretaries. He knew that it was a logical use of his scholarly skills, but in his heart, he admitted to himself that he had fancied himself in a more active role, more in keeping with the dashing charges he had practiced with his cousins in Virginia. And sometimes he was jealous of his brothers and Silas.

Quentin's musical talent made him uniquely valuable, and he was one of the best fifers in the army. There hadn't been much call for musical commands yet, but everyone knew how important they would be when the joint militias went to battle. Some of the musicians were so young, their mothers had followed them to camp, but Quentin, with his usual self-sufficiency, thrived on army life. He missed his family in Boston, but even that was in a matter-of-fact way. Having made the decision to run away to join the army had settled the affair for him. And to be able to indulge his passion for music for a useful cause added much to his contentment.

"He is the best soldier of all of us," Justin observed. "But then, I should have guessed he would be. I have never known Quentin to do anything shabbily once he's set his mind to it."

Justin was also on Washington's staff, but he, even more than Ad, chafed at the sedentary duties. To his relief, Washington had allowed him to go with Silas, Henry Knox and Henry's brother William on the expedition to Fort Ticonderoga to bring back the guns. He, Silas, and Henry were friendly business rivals from their bookstore days and compatriots from their involvement in the militia, in the Boston Grenadier Corps. And they all shared a good reading knowledge of military tactics, including the deployment of artillery. While that might not be as useful as experience gained on the battlefield, for the Continental Army with its citizen-soldiers plus a sprinkling of veterans of the French and Indian War, any kind of knowledge was valued.

Justin could hardly wait to tell Sarah about the grueling journey to and from the old fort, or how they had pulled the guns on sleighs over every kind of terrain, how the cold and the hardship had meant little against the knowledge that the guns would surely free Boston from the redcoats.

For Silas, the journey had been a revelation. Justin and Ad would have given up their favored positions with Washington if they were unable to secure a like place for him. But he didn't want one. Justin and Ad treated him as a brother, but he was keenly aware that he was not. And though Washington was, in the main, a self-taught man, most of the young officers who surrounded him were highly educated and from prominent families. Silas did not want to pretend to be of their rank.

In Henry Knox's mission, Silas found salvation without guilt. He and Henry had discussed artillery often and at length before the war began, while Silas had worked for Marcus and Henry had presided over his own bookstore. And they both believed that no matter how valorous one's troops, if they faced artillery without cannon of their own, they could not prevail.

Silas doubted he would be able to explain it to Addie, but the big guns fascinated him with their deadly promise—cumbersome, cold, and inert, until they caught fire and thundered over the battlefield, their sound and smoke as terrifying as the killing blows of their shot. And even if he could explain the awe he felt, he would never attempt to defend the affection that had grown as the heavy ordnance was trundled over rough, frozen land until he had begun silently to urge the cannon on as if they were another race of soldiers.

Sometimes Silas felt a ripple of unease at how readily he had taken to being a soldier, at how much beauty he found in the possibilities of destruction. Quentin's calm acceptance of this new life was somewhat defensible on the grounds of the music he created, though that music was to be used to direct battles. Silas reminded himself that he had always been interested in his father's life as a soldier. He wished his father had lived long enough so that he could have asked him about his days in the militia. He wondered if his father had thought his life well spent in helping to break the power of the French and their Indian allies.

He also wondered if he would seem much changed to Addie or she to him. He imagined their reunion in various ways, always cautioning himself that she might not be there. He could not bring himself to face the fact that Marcus would surely be gone. Marcus had been as much of a father to Silas as he would allow, and he had hoped, despite the odds against it, that there would be some reconciliation between them, even though he had joined the Patriot cause.

*

Any temptation the British might have felt to delay was vanquished by Washington's fortifying of Foster's Hill on the Dorchester Neck. This position allowed his artillery to be pointed at the docks and wharves. The British were out of the town by March 17, though their ships still lingered in the harbor. It was a sight to behold with more than a hundred vessels of varying sizes riding the water. They carried some nine thousand men and officers, plus nearly a thousand of their women and children, and more than eleven hundred Loyalists. The ships finally set sail on March 27.

When Continental troops approached the British outposts to enter the city, they thought sentinels yet remained, but to their amusement, they discovered that the redcoats had constructed whimsical effigies, complete with paper ruffles and horseshoe ornaments, to take their places.

Washington could have staged a triumphant parade into the city, but instead he visited quietly and surveyed the damage the occupying troops had done to the city during the siege. He ordered British fortifications destroyed. He and his general officers attended a thanksgiving service, and then he left to proceed south with his troops.

The Valencourts and Silas entered the city with Washington's party, but they had their commander's leave to attend to their family affairs and his order that they rejoin the army as soon as possible. In addition, Silas had the general's permission to marry Addie—if she was still there.

"She is of age, and her brothers assure me that it is her wish to marry you," the general said. "In these troubled times, it is my privilege to command joy." The general's smile had given Silas a glimpse of the genial man Washington must have been before he had shouldered the burden of leading the Continental Army.

As the young men got their first look at the changes in the town, they were struck immediately by the desolation—trees, fences, even buildings missing, having been chopped down for firewood, and furnishings and shop goods, such as they were after so long without trade, strewn about the streets.

Since it was on the way and guessing that Sarah would be with Addie, Justin decided to check for his wife at the Valencourt house before he went on to his own home.

Now that reunion was close at hand, they were all nervous. Even Quentin's habitual calm was faltering.

"I know Addie must have been angry when I ran away. I hope she isn't any more."

"I think she'll be so happy to see us, nothing else will matter," Ad said. Though Justin and Silas had their doubts, Ad continued to be certain that neither Sarah nor Addie had left with the enemy.

But of all the homecomings they had imagined, none of them had pictured Addie as they found her.

She and Tullia met them at the door, and Ad barely restrained a gasp at the change in his twin. She was so thin, she looked like a child rather than a young woman, but her eyes were old and weary in her pale face.

"Thank God!" she exclaimed as she saw that they were all there before her, but even as she opened her arms to them, the shadows did not lift from her eyes.

"Is Sarah with you?" Justin asked as he hugged his sister, looking over her shoulder and past Tullia.

"No, she's not here." Addie's throat tightened, and she was not sure she could go on. The moment she had dreaded was upon her, tainting the joy of having her brothers and Silas with her again. She heard Tullia sniffing back tears and knew there was no help to be had in that quarter.

"Then I'd better be off to our house," Justin said, but as her disquiet became his, he asked, "Surely she didn't leave with the British?"

"No. Oh, Justin, Sarah died some weeks ago, of smallpox. I tried to save her, but she was too sick."

Justin and the others stared at her as if she had spoken in a foreign language none understood. The worst thing Justin had imagined was that Sarah, out of filial obligation, might have felt compelled to go with the Goodwins if they left. That she, rather than he, might become a casualty of war had not occurred to him.

"I'm sorry, so sorry," Addie whispered, and she was so frail standing there, trembling, that Ad moved to support her, but Silas was quicker, putting his arms around her, drawing her close to his strength, not caring that all could see.

It struck him like a physical blow that as Sarah had died, so too Addie could have perished before he returned to her. "Addie, sweetheart, Justin knows, we all know, no one could have cared better for Sarah than you."

Quentin and Ad moved to flank their brother, but it was Tullia who, regaining control of her emotions, led them all deeper into the house where she could watch over them and offer the basic comforts of food and warmth.

Quentin stopped in his tracks and cocked his head as if listening for some faint, distant sound. "Papa, Mary, and the children are gone, aren't they?" he asked, but it wasn't really a question, and he didn't need his sister's nod to know the answer.

They settled on the benches around Tullia's kitchen table as Addie explained, "The Goodwins left, too. Papa wanted to believe that they would return soon, but Mary convinced him to set his affairs in order before they sailed." Having spoken of Sarah's death, Addie found the rest easy to relate, and she did so in a monotone, as if giving the details of someone else's life. And she noted that her brothers, like her, felt no outrage over the arrangements Marcus had made.

"Papa has been most generous to us," Ad said.

"Mary has also, at least to me," Addie told him. "She left a letter for me. She deeded her farm to me, to keep or sell as I wish. Even if Papa is still denying it, Mary knows it is unlikely they will return. She wrote that if any of her children ever do, she will trust that we will welcome them."

She watched her brothers' faces, watched them struggling to accept all that had happened in their absence, and her heart ached for them. At least she had been with Sarah until the last moment, and she had been able to bid their father, Mary, and the children farewell, face to face, no matter how difficult it had been. The words had been hard to say, but she and her father had made peace.

"Papa loves you all, including you, Silas, and he is proud of you. He asked me to tell you that. And Peter wants you to be happy. He wanted you to know that he will miss you."

Justin was too shocked to express any feelings yet, and Ad struggled to suppress his grief, but Quentin's eyes filled with tears, and he bowed his head, his youth for once overcoming his self-possession.

Addie became aware that Silas still had his arms around her as they sat together, that his warmth and strength were stealing into the cold, bleak places in her soul. He was leaner than he had been before, and his skin was more weathered, but the essence of him was blessedly the same. She looked at his strong hands holding hers, and she felt secure for the first time since he had left nearly a year ago. She had feared that in spite of his loving messages, they might feel awkward when they saw each other again. But the raw emotions of the reunion had stripped away hesitation.

Boston no longer seemed like home, but Silas did. She laced her fingers with his and welcomed the gentle pressure of reassurance he gave her.

"I wanted to thank Sarah for sending the silver spoons with me. I managed to save one, just a small one, to bring back to her, but the others we used for money." Justin fumbled in his pocket and found the teaspoon carefully wrapped in a handkerchief. He stared at it as if he no longer recognized what it was. "Maybe it was bad luck that I took them." He was like a child taking the blame for a catastrophe that was none of the child's doing.

"She wanted you to take them," Addie told him patiently, as if the question of the silver spoons had to be settled. She didn't know what else to do.

"Nothing was as important to Sarah as you were," Silas said. "You must remember that above all else."

"She was so beautiful. If I ever marry, I would like a wife just like Sarah," Quentin observed earnestly.

"She took her studies very seriously. She wanted to be able to share your interests in all sorts of subjects," Addie said. "And I could not have asked for a better sister."

"She was good help in this house when we took in wounded redcoats. She didn't like them, but she thought maybe if she cared for the enemy, then the enemy would care for you if you were hurt," Tullia explained.

One by one they offered their tributes to Justin, as if they were having a service for Sarah, in place of the small, private one Justin had missed.

"Thank you. I am going to our house now." He looked at Addie, who assured him that nothing had been changed there. Then he said, "I do not want anyone to go with me."

"General Washington needs every man," Silas reminded him quietly, and Justin met his eyes squarely. "I know. I will not fail him." *As I failed Sarah* were words unspoken but loud in his mind.

Addie was so intent on the exchange between Justin and Silas, she did not notice that Tullia was herding Quentin and Ad away until, when Justin left, she and Silas were alone.

"Addie, I… I imagined this very differently, but—"

She interrupted him. "Silas, do you love me?"

"God, yes! More than ever before, and it was too much then."

"I love you, too. And I don't want to wait any longer. Will you marry me?"

All the reasons he had once thought so valid for delaying the marriage slipped through his mind once more but vanished like smoke in face of the reality of her in his arms. And in defiance of the sorrow of the day, he found himself laughing.

He stood and pulled her to her feet, smiling down at her. "Oh, Addie mine! Yes, I'll marry you. I have no prospects, but I do have General Washington's permission."

"Then you had better do the proper thing." She laughed with him, and then she said softly, "We have Papa's permission, too. He knows we will care for each other."

She looked up into his face, closing her eyes as he bent his head to kiss her. His mouth was warm and firm and tender, and this was not like the other stolen kisses. Though his muscles tensed with the effort of self-restraint, he kissed her as if they had all the time in the world, as if there were no war, as if Sarah's death and Marcus's departure did not shadow them. His mouth tasted, teased, and promised, while his hands held and stroked her, invisibly marking her as his own.

Addie felt a strange tide sweeping through her, sending streams of heat that reached to the tips of her fingers and toes and made her feel giddy and young, as she had never expected to feel again. Her last coherent thought was that this was what war meant, feeling so much at once —joy and sorrow, hope and despair—until all the emotions merged into a fierce celebration of life.

Chapter 12

Addie and Silas were married by a minister who was also an artillery-man, which seemed a fitting coda to the day. And Henry Knox, over six feet tall and heavily built, honored them with his cheerful presence by stopping by just long enough to witness their exchange of vows. He, too, was married to a daughter of Loyalists, his wife's parents having left as had Marcus. He and his wife Lucy were devoted to each other, so it was as if he were offering Silas and Addie the reassurance of his experience.

Under the circumstances, Addie would have foregone any celebration beyond the simple service itself, but Tullia insisted there would be a wedding supper. "Mistress Sarah would want it for you," she said firmly, "and Justin does, too. War or no war, sorrow or not, this is the beginning of your married life."

Indeed, Justin was doing his best to control his grief. Whatever tears he had shed had been in private in the house he had shared with his wife. There wasn't time for mourning. The men had to rejoin the army, and there was a host of matters to settle before they left.

But for the moment, they shared the wedding feast Tullia, with Addie's help, had prepared from what remained in the larder. With much of the Patriot population coming back into the city, and with the way open for trade with the countryside, food was starting to flow in again, but it would take a while before the markets were operating smoothly once more.

Although the weather was cool for it, Addie wore the cream silk gown embroidered with flowers that she had worn to the dance at Castleton and had brought back with her. The dress had needed to be taken in here and there, tied tighter in other spots due to the weight she had lost during the siege, but she and Tullia had done a quick job of it. When Silas saw her in it, the delight in his eyes was approval enough.

Ad had been very proud as he substituted for Marcus in giving the bride into Silas's keeping, but he had known it was actually his twin who was doing the giving of herself. Silas had appeared far more nervous than she. Ad caught her eye across the dining table, and she flashed him a saucy grin. He loved his brothers and Silas, but Addie was part of him and he of her. And he knew her well enough to know she had some scheme in mind, but it was Silas, not he, who would have to contend with whatever she planned.

Addie enjoyed the little gathering, albeit keeping an anxious eye on Justin, fearing the celebration might prove too great a strain on him. But aside from an air of abstraction that made him miss the train of conversation now and then, he had himself well in hand.

Addie's brothers had had word from Castleton, and that provided one of the main topics of discussion. Sissy and the aunts were fine, and the men too, with Uncle Hartley continuing his work with the Continental Congress while Hart, Reese, and Sissy's husband, James, were serving with the Virginia militia.

When Governor Dunmore had fled Williamsburg to escape Patriot fervor, he had not sailed for England but had established himself on his warship with the intention of organizing Loyalists to sweep away all Rebels in the colony. Using a flotilla of boats manned by British regulars and Loyalists, he continued to launch raids against the Tidewater plantations. Even Mount Vernon, General Washington's home, was said to be threatened.

Lord Dunmore had also offered freedom to all slaves who would come in to the British side, enraging the planters.

And Lord Dunmore's wooing of the slaves was not Virginia's only problem, because in December the King and Parliament had issued an order that all trade and intercourse with the colonies be prohibited, and they had authorized the seizing of American ships. This was hard enough on New England and the Mid-Atlantic colonies, which had some manufactories of their own, but for Virginia and the other Southern colonies, it was devastating, so dependent were they on imported goods. The fact that the decree was expected did not make it less onerous.

As serious as these British actions were, Virginia's worst wound had been inflicted by the death of Peyton Randolph. For so long the most important man in Virginia politics and then in the Continental Congress, he had had a fatal attack of apoplexy brought on by the press of too much work. Virginians of every station in life mourned him, and the Valencourts knew how personal the loss would be for their uncle who had worked long years with Mr. Randolph. And the Randolphs, like the Valencourts, clearly demonstrated the tragedy of civil war, for though Peyton had died a Patriot, his brother John had taken ship for England, his Loyalist views having made him increasingly unpopular. His wife and two daughters had accompanied him, but not his son Edmund. Edmund was serving in the Continental Army.

"Hart and Reeves want to come north to join the army, and Harry Lee is of the same mind," Ad said. "But they are needed still in Virginia. In any case, they are serving as dragoons, and for all his liking for fine horseflesh, General Washington doesn't see much use for cavalry yet." The wistful tone in his voice betrayed how easily he could picture himself as a dragoon. Most officers rode horseback in the field, but that was not the same as being part of the thunder and dash of a mounted troop.

Addie was tempted to broach the subject of their plans, hers in particular, but she decided it would be better done after this night. The hour was advancing, and she struggled to hide her amusement as she watched the knowledge dawn on her brothers that this was, after all, their sister's wedding night and that they ought to leave her and Silas alone. They were clumsy in their attempts to exit gracefully.

"I have... er, some music to practice," Quentin announced abruptly, and his face flushed scarlet.

"I have some reading to do." Justin rose so swiftly from his chair, he nearly knocked it over.

"I... I have... Oh, hell! Good night, Addie and Silas." Ad kissed his laughing sister on the cheek and sketched a little bow to Silas.

As at their wedding, it was Silas who was nervous as he and Addie went upstairs to the chamber that had been Marcus and Mary's, a room more fitting, according to Tullia, for a bridal chamber than Addie's virginal quarters. And laid out on the big bed were a nightgown, also part of the Virginia wardrobe, for Addie and a bed shirt for Silas.

Addie touched the fine cambric of the gown and smiled. "Tullia obviously trusts that you will keep me warm."

The light cast by candles and the fire in the hearth was shadowy, but Addie could see Silas's swarthy skin darken further.

"Do I embarrass you with my boldness?" she asked, genuinely curious and wondering if she was going to have to change her ways a great deal in order to be a suitable wife for Silas.

"No, sweetheart, never! Your boldness delights me! It is just that…" He paused, searching for the words, and decided on the truth. "Addie, I have never wanted any woman as much as I want you. I have never loved another. I haven't had much experience, and I don't want to frighten you or do anything wrong." He thought about the prostitute he had visited once, but he didn't think that was part of the truth Addie needed to know. He and Justin had gone to the Mount Whoredom section of the town, both of them scared but egging each other on. And as such encounters went, they had been lucky—the women had been professionals, but they had also been appreciative of two handsome young men and had taken a little extra time to tutor so that they might have their own "bit a sport." As far as Silas could recall, time seemed to have been the most important ingredient of the whole exercise. It seemed precious little to know at this point, but it would have to do.

"Will you play lady's maid?" Addie asked. "I have dressed so well for our wedding day, I must have your help or summon someone else."

"This part I can do." Silas laughed with the sudden release of tension. Addie's calm acceptance of his presence and of what was to come was as entrancing as if she were dancing ancient patterns with his soul, making him part of a celebration of life eons older than either of them.

"Time," he reminded himself silently, "time," and he undid the intricate fastenings of the gown with slow care, stopping to touch the soft flesh he revealed. He touched with just the tips of his fingers, then with his lips—at the bend of an elbow, at the curve of her neck where it met her shoulder, along the rim of an ear, at the top of her spine and down, until Addie was shivering with the sensations he conjured from her skin, and he was leading the dance.

"Ariadne, my love." He used her given name as if he were repeating their wedding vows, and despite the effects of the siege that had left her so fragile, she was perfect to him. He swept her up in his arms and tucked her into the bed before she could take a chill, and then he stripped off his clothes and lay down beside her, the nightclothes forgotten.

Addie had only a brief glimpse of his body as he stood beside the bed, but it was enough to make her draw an audible breath.

"Are you afraid?" he asked as he settled beside her, knowing she had seen his arousal. Still determined not to rush her, he held himself apart, not crowding her.

It was she who cuddled close, putting her arms around him. "I am not afraid. I think 'awed' would be a more accurate term." The male body was not foreign to her. She had often seen naked slaves in Virginia, and caring for the sick and wounded meant that modesty could not always be preserved. But none of that meant anything because she had not gazed on their flesh with desire.

Her breath caught again as she stroked the strong muscles of his back. "How beautiful you are." Her lips were soft against his shoulder, her voice stirring against his skin like butterfly wings. "Silas, my love, my husband."

Addie's words excited Silas as much as her touch, and he began to kiss and caress her in counterpoint until they were both feverish with the dance. Even when he moved over her, urging her legs farther apart, she showed no fear. He groaned aloud as he entered her; she was so tight and hot, his resolution to go slowly wavered. "I don't want to hurt you!"

She answered his harsh cry by gripping his corded buttocks and taking him deeper. He was big and hard inside of her, stretching her until she burned with it, piercing her maidenhead with a sharp thrust, sharp pain. But the hurt didn't matter, mixing and soaring with the passion that was itself kin to pain until she could not tell where the borders began or ended. All of it made her feel more alive than she had since Captain Byrne had died, since Sarah had died. Pain was a small price to pay to feel her heart, her body, and her soul again.

Silas's face was wild in the flickering light; his eyes glittered, and his lips were drawn back in a feral snarl as he surrendered to the demands of his body, surrendered to her. Addie understood that her own response, slowed by pain, was not so overwhelming as his, and even that she welcomed because it enabled her to witness what she was giving to him.

He collapsed on her, heaving as he fought for air. He rolled to his side, leaving her. And when he had the breath for it, he said, "I'm sorry. It went too fast, too damn fast." He had truly believed he could control himself; his limited experience had not warned him that he could be swept away completely by the tide of his passion. He dreaded that he had spoiled intimacy for Addie, that he had violated not only her maidenhead, but also her trust.

"Not too fast, husband—perfect." Addie's languorous voice soothed his fear, and she moved to lie half over him, her body still trusting his.

At that moment, Silas felt as loved as he ever had in his life, and tears pricked his eyes. His arms came around her, holding her close to his heart.

Instinctively, Addie knew that making love with Silas would grow easier and more pleasurable physically as her body became accustomed to his, but she doubted she could ever feel closer to him than she did now, and giving him the joy she had felt vibrating through his body was power she had never imagined. For her, it had been perfect.

Addie thought Silas had fallen asleep, but then he said, "I was afraid you would leave with your father. I was more afraid that you would leave as the wife of Captain Byrne."

He felt the tremor that ran through her before she spoke. "Captain Byrne died in this house, in my arms." She described how it had been, how she had watched a strong young man fade into death.

"He loved you."

"Yes, he did. He left me his ring, to remember him, and I will keep it for that. But I don't want you to think it is for any other reason.

Captain Byrne's feelings were his own. I liked him very much, but he knew I loved you."

She made Silas feel secure enough so that he could spare regret for the captain's death. And he could not escape the knowledge that in war, harsh fate was even more random and active than usual. It could easily have been he who had died and the captain who had lived to console Addie.

"When we got your Christmas messages, you weren't in Cambridge, were you? You were going after Fort Ti's guns." Silas and Justin had talked about the journey, but only now did Addie consider that those messages she and Sarah had received must have been written before the men had left.

Silas confirmed it. "Ad made sure they got to you, with the General's permission, of course."

Addie shivered and held him tighter, more determined than ever that they not be separated again. In sleep, they still clung to each other until he eased away from her in the early hours of the morning to add wood to the fire.

She awakened as soon as he left her, and she watched as the fire blazed up and illuminated him. He turned when he felt her eyes on him. She stretched luxuriously and continued to gaze at him without shame.

He grinned at her. "You look like a contented cat, Mistress Bradwell."

"I feel like a contented wife—a very, very fortunate wife." Her eyes continued to enjoy the sight of him until he was too close, and then she didn't need to look at him any more because he was over her, touching her everywhere, and when he entered her, her body knew him and rejoiced. The soreness from the first time didn't matter; she was swept away with him.

In the light of morning, with the stains of her virginity a battle flag on the bed linens, she announced her plan. "Tullia and I are going to go with you and my brothers."

Silas froze in the act of donning his shirt and stared at Addie. She was sitting on the bed, finally wearing the nightgown, and she looked so delicate and feminine, he was distracted and wondered if he had heard her aright.

Her eyes were more gold than brown, catching light as she stared back at him. "I mean it. Tullia and I are going to go with you. Or more specifically, we will follow you because there are many affairs to complete here first, and you must rejoin the army."

"But I thought—"

"You thought I would stay in Boston and wait again? I will not! This city means naught but death to me now, and to Tullia. There is no more family left, no reason to stay. You are my family now, and I will not be separated from you for days, weeks, months on end."

Silas started to ask if she also intended to take the field with him but thought better of it. Too easily, he could picture her dressed as a boy, as she had so often done when she and her twin were up to some devilment, and it wasn't too long a stretch to add a weapon to the image.

"You could go to Virginia." It sounded weak to his ears.

"Yes, I could, but I won't because you won't be there."

Silas considered himself a man of reason; Marcus had taught him to be so. But reason had never seemed to have much to do with his love for Addie, and it had less power now that he knew her body's response to his. Worst of all, he could not deny that she had faced as much hazard and death as he in these past months. There was no guarantee that leaving her in Boston or persuading her to go to Virginia would keep her safe. His best hope was that her brothers would direct her on some safe course. But they disappointed him. They, no more than he, were proof against her determination, especially with Tullia supporting her, and beyond that, they felt that any power to guide Addie's life was now vested in her husband.

"As if we were ever able to change her mind anyway," Ad muttered to Justin. Yet, as Addie's twin, he felt obliged to point out the rigors of camp life. "It's truly no place for women, and the general is trying to discourage women and children from following the army."

"Including his wife?" Addie asked sweetly.

Mistress Washington, or "Lady Washington" as some now called her, had been with the general during most of his stay in Cambridge, and she had left from there to go to New York where the General would meet her after his visit to Boston. Other officers' wives had been at Cambridge, too, so Ad had to concede the point, but he persevered. "The general's lady and other officers' wives will surely go home once the campaign is underway."

"Certainly not all the women will go; they are not all officers' wives."

"What do you and Tullia plan to do about this house?" Justin asked.

"It is as much your responsibility as mine," Addie reminded him calmly. "But if you all agree, my plan would be to sell the most valuable articles, if we can. And the silver Papa left for us can be used for coin. Other things may not yield so ready a profit, but we can try. Then we can rent the house. People are coming back into the town, and many buildings have been damaged. There will be need of fine residences such as this. I intend that Mary's farm go on as usual, with its tenants in place. We know honest men who will serve as our agents and bankers; they did not all leave with Papa. I assume the Continental Army is no different from any other; you will need the means to equip yourselves as officers."

They could not dispute her on this because she was correct, and the more formal the shape of the army became, the more demand there was for personal investment by the men who would lead others. Money was needed for arms, uniforms, horses, for food, and if one wished to lead one's own company, then money must be forthcoming for the recruitment. While the Congress might declare itself in support of the army it had created, the problem of raising funds from the various colonies was already proving serious. Some colonies sent units that were well equipped; others sent those that were in need of everything. And no matter what colony he came from, a man without money had little chance of being more than a common soldier.

"Life around the army isn't very tidy," Quentin said, as if that would surely be the deciding factor for his sister.

"I wager it's a good deal tidier since the women arrived," she retorted, and Quentin had the grace to look abashed, confirming her speculation.

It threw the brothers off balance to have Marcus gone and Tullia siding with Addie. In many other households it would have been easy to issue an order to their sister and expect it to be obeyed, but neither she nor they had been raised that way. Addie was as strong-willed, as educated, and as resourceful as any one of them. The only thing she lacked was their physical strength, and Quentin, for one, wasn't sure he would want to test that were she in a full temper.

Justin's knowledge that he was the eldest and therefore should be the one to take charge was tempered by Addie's marriage to Silas and, more, by the haunting idea that Sarah might have survived had she been with him instead of in the town.

Ad felt the most responsibility, as if by being her twin and sharing childhood so closely with her he had led her astray.

Addie studied their faces. "I hope you do not gamble much in games of chance, for your faces betray you. I am Silas's wife, but I am also my own woman. I have been so for a long time. Would you want me changed, even to keep me safe?"

It was an honest question asking for no less in the answer, and one by one, they answered, "No."

"Then we have nothing more to discuss except how best to settle our affairs here."

Addie began to spread out lists and inventories, and Justin whispered to Silas, "God grant that the British do not have so fine a strategist among their generals."

The planning went smoothly until the Valencourts discussed shares.

Silas thought they were correct in allotting money for Tullia, for her to use as she saw fit, though Marcus had left her something.

"Her loyalty to us is without question, and now that she has thrown her lot in with us, she should be able to support herself easily away from us if the time comes," Justin said, and his siblings agreed. Then he said, "My brothers and I have decided that whatever was left here for us, if there was anything at all, would be shared equally among the five of us."

It took Silas a moment to understand that they were counting him as one of the Valencourts. Rather than being pleased, he was horrified. "You cannot do this! It is wrong!"

"No, it is quite proper," Justin countered. "Papa treated you as his son. We regard you as our brother, more than ever now that you are married to Addie. In sharing with you, we share with her. Two Bradwells plus three Valencourts equals five. It is a simple equation."

Silas opened his mouth and closed it again, unable to speak for the lump in his throat, and Addie's eyes filled with tears. She loved her brothers dearly, but she had not expected such generosity from them and would have judged it fair had they expected her portion to suffice for Silas.

Then Justin shocked them all by adding, "We will all share whatever I can raise from the sale of my house and furnishings." He raised his hand to forestall protest. "Before, it was different. Sarah had become my family. Now Sarah is gone, and you are my family once again. And I would never live in that house again, never." The vehemence in his low voice made Addie's heart ache for him, and she understood that acting as head of the family in some way assuaged his grief.

They had avoided talking about the bookstore and printing office, and Addie had avoided visiting them since she had learned they were to be Darius's, but Justin brought up this subject, too. "Darius will not be pleased if he ever comes to take possession. There is little left, and the staff has fled. The buildings look well enough on the outside, though a few panes of glass are broken, but inside, well, it is a good thing the press and type have been stored away." Addie had told him that much and that it was Mary who had suggested this precaution. "The interior destruction may have been part of the plan that nothing of use to our cause remain in the town, or perhaps it was done for nothing more than resentment against Papa's support of the government. There are a few books remaining, but I suppose..."

He glanced at his sister, and she confirmed his suspicion.

"Papa had begun to sell his library."

It was not really a surprise because they had noticed the empty shelves, but all of the men were somber, thinking of how much Marcus had loved his books.

Justin cleared his throat and went on. "As for the wharfage and other properties, there is nothing we can do, except to try to leave them protected in our absence. We have no legal claim to them. It is up to Darius to use them or dispose of them." He flexed his shoulders to release the tension in them. "I do not fault Papa for what he has done, but I regret that most of what he worked so hard to build might be lost. Darius is as staunch a Tory as Papa. He will have little claim here unless we lose the fight. And that, with Providence willing and General Washington leading us, will not happen."

He put out his hand, and one by one they added theirs.

"To Liberty or Death," Justin said.

No one questioned Addie's right to make the pledge.

Made in the USA
Columbia, SC
31 May 2022

61132376R00107